Kate Irving

Clear Light from the Spirit World

Kate Irving

Clear Light from the Spirit World

ISBN/EAN: 9783337269357

Printed in Europe, USA, Canada, Australia, Japan

Cover: Foto ©Andreas Hilbeck / pixelio.de

More available books at **www.hansebooks.com**

CLEAR LIGHT

FROM THE

SPIRIT WORLD.

BY

KATE IRVING.

NEW YORK:

G. W. Carleton & Co., Publishers.

LONDON: S. LOW, SON & CO.

Dedication.

THIS RECORD OF FACTS, IN MY OWN EXPERIENCE, IS AFFEC-
TIONATELY INSCRIBED TO DEPARTED FRIENDS I HAVE
LOVED IN OUR HOMES HERE, AND WHOM I AM
TO MEET IN THEIR HOMES IN THE
SPIRIT-LAND HEREAFTER,

AND ALSO TO MY FRIENDS NOW LIVING ON EARTH, WHO,
THROUGH SO MANY UNSATISFIED YEARS, HAVE NOT YET
FOUND THE REPOSE FOR WHICH THEY ARE STILL
LONGING, AND WHICH I FEEL SURE IS
WITHIN THEIR REACH.

AFFECTIONATELY,

KATE IRVING.

CONTENTS.

vi CONTENTS.

I.

LIKE everybody else, in Christian lands, I had always been taught that we live after we cease to live here; and I thought I believed it. I *hoped* it was true, but I wanted to *know* it for myself. Faith was not enough to satisfy me on so vast, so vital, so infinite a subject. · I read and listened and wanted to believe, and I tried to be satisfied. But I could not rest, for I could not stop thinking.

I might perhaps have found repose had I not been brought up in the chilling creed of the old New England theology. But I could not accept it. My *heart* turned from its fearful dogmas with indescribable horror. The thought that it *might* be true spread such gloom over the endless future life for me, and to so many dear ones, that

I dreaded the very idea of living forever ! To be helplessly immortal seemed a cruel doom !

With such an early education I could not have a very sunny childhood, and my girlhood was gloomier still. Gradually the light of the morning of my life faded away and at last it seemed to go out. I was left in so deep a state of rayless gloom that existence was robbed of its charm and became a curse.

In some sad and mysterious way, music, which had once entranced my soul, had become powerless even to soothe me, my passion for flowers was dead, and the warm embrace of loving friends, which once thrilled me with rapture, now chilled me with dreadful forebodings. Behind the gorgeous sunsets, with all their blended tints and hues of ravishing beauty, I saw leaden skies darkening into clouds of inky blackness. Everywhere, in every scene my whole being was penetrated with the awful consciousness that I was a helpless, doomed victim of " wrath in the hands of an angry God ! "

How long this state of mind could have lasted without driving me to insanity I cannot even now tell. I only distinctly recall one evening, while taking my solitary walk on the bank of the lovely stream which skirted the eastern border of our garden, that the thought flashed on me that I was *going mad*. My soul revolted from the idea with horror.

I began to come to myself, and inquire if I had not cowardly surrendered myself body and spirit to the guidance of others, who had instilled into my mind a dreadful creed which no reasoning being could accept.

As suddenly light flashed into my innermost mind, and I began to feel the tight cords that had bound my soul loosen, and a new and delicious sense of freedom came over me, to which I had from childhood been a stranger. I felt weak in this new life of reason, but I felt strong enough never to be so enslaved again. Something dreadful *might* happen, but I would not die mad, nor take one step farther on the road which had been leading me there.

I looked off on the shining river, away beyond its green banks, over the enamelled fields, and still farther, where the wooded hills lost themselves in the rosy sunset and the evening star was beaming in its silver light, and I felt a new inspiration steal warmly into my *heart*. The fetters of a hard bondage fell from my weary limbs, and I looked around me expecting still to find myself enveloped by the blinding mists of the old superstition ! But those mists had dissolved, and gazing far up into the stellar universe, as I fell to my knees I cried out in an agony of imploration :

"Oh! if there be an infinite Father, let Him pity his poor child ! "

I bore that answer to my prayer home with me to my chamber, which seemed a new room and a new world.

I had long kept my feelings to myself as far as I could, and yet every one who knew me had noted how changed I had become since later years. My constitution, inherited and cared for so well, had not been impaired ; and no one had ever suspected how deeply or keenly I had suffered.

But now they all saw—they could not help seeing, nor did I think of concealing it—the emancipation from thraldom and suffering through which I had passed. Descending to the parlor later in the evening, I opened the long-neglected piano, and struck the plaintive air of Mrs Hemans' "Messenger Bird":

"Tell us, thou bird of the solemn strain,
  Can those we have loved forget?"

It was an early summer evening and all the windows were open. Neighboring friends dropped in, and we sang and played some of the old familiar songs of other days, and everyone felt a cheerfulness that had not been witnessed there for a long time. The secret probably was known to myself alone.

In parting for the night with my old home companion, who went to the stair with me to give and take the last kiss, she said:

"Kate, you seem happier to-night than I have seen you for a long, long time. Are you?"

"I am, dearest friend."

"Bless God, my child; you do not know what a load you have taken from my heart."

Blessed friend! How little you then divined

the change that had come over me.   Nor did she know it fully until long afterward ; for she had been educated in a still darker generation, when that terrible creed still held, but with relaxing strength, the intellect and conscience of New England in its merciless grasp.

II.

THE FIRST NIGHT OF MY NEW LIFE.

IT was the beginning of a new life for me. I had never fully known before what that wonderful word *Life* meant. It was years ago, and, much as I have learned since, I feel so incompetent to define it now that I can only invoke the forbearance of the wiser of my readers, and the patience of my less experienced ones, while I lay before them as plain and unvarnished an account as I can give of the way I travelled from the desert land of doubt and misery to the peaceful country where I now dwell.

It is not a long story, nor will it, I trust, be an unattractive one to the reader. I really have nothing so very wonderful, strange, or extraordinary to tell. Thousands could relate, and thousands have told stranger things than I shall, but my heart goes out with a warm desire to shed over the lives of others some of the blessed rays which have illuminated my own.

I sat long by the window, glad to be alone. And yet I did not *feel* alone ; even the moonlight was full of living sympathy. Yes, even with *me*, who had so long been shut out from all glad thoughts of earth ; above all, from glad thoughts of the black, bewildering universe with which I had hitherto been wildly floating—for I knew I was floating, moving on somewhere, I knew not whither.

The moon was sailing high and full in the azure heavens, and the words of Dr. Beattie, so familiar in school-girl lessons, came to me with a new and half-sad meaning :

" Roll on thou fair orb, and with gladness pursue
   The path which conducts thee to splendor again ;
But man's faded glory, what change shall renew !
   Ah ! fool to exult in a glory so vain."

"No !" my soul, my whole self exclaimed ; " that cannot be so. Not to live hereafter ! not to live forever ! It cannot, cannot be. Thou, my immortal, cannot die. But where shall I go, or whither fly when death shall set thee free ?"

It was the first time the dread spectre of annihilation in all its ghastly hideousness had ever appeared before me. I recoiled from its presence as I would from the hiss of a serpent.

I looked on the fair face of the moon again and I grew calm. Strains of music came floating on the still air. I listened to hear where they came from, but I could not tell; all I could know was that the music surrounded me on all sides, and yet I thought everybody must hear it. It was different from any music I had ever heard. Something like it had sometimes come to me in delicious dreams, from which I woke with tears as I opened my eyes to the morning sun and went to the weary work of another day's thinking.

At last the music grew fainter and fainter, till it died away far up in the night sky. I did not dare to believe that it came from a higher, a better world, although I was sure it did not come from earth. I said to myself:

"It makes me happy, and oh! I am glad. Who knows but that, after all, there may be something in the wonderful accounts, now becoming so common, of celestial influences reaching earth's inhabitants, as we read of in the Bible and other books. If these things were true *then*, why should they not occur again ?   If they did, is it impossible now ?   Have I not been taught to believe stranger things ? "

I went to my pillow with no reluctance, for I had so long dreaded those sleepless nights that it was with strange surprise that none of the old apprehensions came back to trouble me.   I lay so restfully I can find no name for it but *peace*, for it was more than rest, more even than " that peace of mind dearer than all."

I had sometimes been considered imaginative and peculiar ; but I had never been accused of the weakness of credulity.   In fact, I often erred in yielding too little, rather than too much, to the marvellous.   This disposition to demand absolute proof of anything that did not commend itself to my reason often, perhaps, exposed me to undeserved censure ; but it saved me from the evils of superstition.   Most of all had I been perplexed, and very early, with the so-called miracu-

lous scenes and events of the Bible. No satisfactory solution of those matters had ever been of-
fered to me—only I must *believe*. I could not and
I did not. Everybody else said they did, and I did
not disturb them. I had what satisfaction there
was in what they called *unbelief*. What years of
mental suffering I passed through before the
true light illuminated my soul! But the dawn
was already breaking. My resolution to investigate fearlessly the whole subject *for myself* was
irrevocably fixed.

2

III.

MY INVESTIGATIONS INTO THE SPIRITUALISM OF THE JEWISH SCRIPTURES.

MY mind had from that evening grown calm, and I began to investigate for myself the problem, then commanding such general attention from many of the most cultured minds in Europe and this country : Do we live after death, and can the fact be demonstrated—not be made very *probable*, but *proved?* If so, how? For I said to myself, as myriads had said before all through historic ages, and as the learned and the uncultured seemed to be asking in our times the same question, if the truth of immortality can be demonstrated as plainly as any other scientific problem, is it not the most important fact for all the living to know?

Next in importance came the question, Can

the living hold clear and satisfactory converse with the departed, and in that way learn their condition in the spirit world ?

This knowledge I was resolved to ascertain, if it took my whole life to do it.

I had no guide to lead me, and must confess I was afraid to ask counsel from those I knew best. But I very naturally went to the Bible, for which I had been taught to feel the deepest reverence, as the sole authority given to man to follow—it being, they said, "the only revealed will of God to the human race."

I was more familiar with it than with any other book, and had been taught to accept it without a question of its infallibility. But I could not possibly accept the interpretation which my teachers put upon it ; and so I had turned from it with incredulity and distress.

And yet a sense of terror crept over me at the thought of differing from the judgment of the learned and the pious friends and teachers around me ; and sometimes I felt that I would be "a castaway," a doomed one ! This dreadful nightmare hung over me even in sleep. I dreamed

I was sailing over a dark ocean together with all the beings I loved on earth. But I did not dare to trust myself any farther on the vessel; and at night I sprang overboard, and was not sorry when I saw that great ship sail on, and lose itself in the gloom, as I slowly and peacefully sank in the deep blue waters.

But I had, on the evening I have described, fixed my purpose, and as the question of communications to mortals from the spirit world was now uppermost in my mind, after breakfast I opened my Bible, and before I left my chamber I had read every account of spiritual visits and apparitions, in the Old and New Testaments. There was no one with which I was not as familiar as with a thrice-told tale. But I read them now, as I would for the first time any new book on record, *simply to get the meaning.*

Beginning with Genesis, I found the following incidents :

1. In the garden of Eden our first parents were in direct communication with the spirit world, and they talked familiarly with God. Man was a living soul—he came forth from the dust, and to

the dust he must return. But it seems that his intercourse with the spirit world was not broken by the so-called Fall.

2. When Hagar was driven into exile from Abram's dwelling, an angel appeared to comfort and guide her into the wilderness, and she became the mother, and her son Ishmael the father of a great and enduring nation.

3. Later the Lord appeared to Abraham in the plains of Mamre, as he sat in the tent door in the heat of the day, and three men stood before him with a mysterious message. The patriarch treated these strange visitors with courteous and reverent oriental hospitality. These angel messengers ate, and delivered their incredible revelation, and turned their steps toward Sodom, and " Abraham went with them to lead them on the way."

4. Then we read that "two angels came to Sodom at even," and appeared to Lot, " and he brought them into his house, and made them a feast, and they did eat." The rest of the record is too dreadful to be told—every Sunday-School scholar knows the story. And while Lot lingered

the angels sent to warn and save him "laid hold upon his hands, and upon the hands of his wife, and upon the hands of his two daughters, and brought them without the city, and said, " Escape for thy life ; look not behind thee, neither stay thou in all the plain ; escape to the mountains, lest thou be consumed."

We all know the fate of the Cities of the Plain. Was not this the work of God, and were not his messengers executive angels in the form of men ? I could not help asking this question.   They were in the shape of men.   They talked like men.   Lot thought they were men.   The Sodomites supposed them to be men.   They ate like men, and —*vanished.*   Could they have been anything but the spirits of former dwellers on the earth returned on the mission to take Lot and his family out of Sodom before it was destroyed ?

5. King Saul was in trouble, for he was about to be assailed by the invincible hosts of the Philistines ; and he inquired of the Lord, who answered him neither by dreams, nor by Urim nor by Prophets.   He then commanded his servants to search out one of the females who had a famil

iar spirit. There was such an one at Endor. But the king had already ordered all such persons to be put to death. But not to violate his own decree, he disguised himself, and taking two men with him went to the woman by night, and asked her to divine unto him by her familiar spirit, and bring up the person he should name. He desired Samuel, and the medium invoked his presence. " An old man cometh up," she said. " He is covered with a mantle. And Saul perceived that it was Samuel." His doom was uttered by Samuel, and the words of the old prophet became true.

I was deeply affected by this account. If the record was worthy of its place in the sacred Scriptures, it was worthy of belief, and the facts appeared to be clearly stated. At the call of this woman who had a familiar spirit Samuel appeared in his own proper person ; for Saul knew him, and recognized him, and they held a conversation together, and it was of vital consequence to Saul.

Could Samuel have appeared in his mortal body, which had gone to dust, or did he not come in his glorious, incorruptible, spirit body? St. Paul says "there is a natural body and there is a spiritual body. It is sown a natural body, it is raised a spiritual body."

I folded the book for a moment and asked, What does all this mean? Everybody knew Samuel had died and been buried. Saul knew it only too well, and he was convinced that Samuel lived after his body had gone to dust. Did not Saul, and all who believed or witnessed the account, learn the great truth of man's immortality so abundantly preached, and proved by Jesus in his own person, ages afterward, when he lived and died and appeared again?

Biblical men say *it was a miracle.* That could not solve the problem for me. There seemed to be no doubt in those ages that the spirits of the departed came back and identified themselves and delivered messages to the living; why should not such things happen now?

I continued my search all through the Old Testament, and closed it with a new but deeper impression of the predominance of the part which angelic agency and spirit inspiration had in the life and history of the Jewish people, and the preservation of the knowledge and worship of the only true God and the life to come.

I then opened the New Testament, where I found the same agency of spirits pervading the whole system of Christianity. Heaven is everywhere represented as the source from which all spiritual influences flowed, and in most instances they came through beings in human form, who used human language, and they distinctly announced the authority with which they were clothed to execute their missions. They announced to Mary and Elizabeth their approaching maternity and made those two mothers glad with a knowledge beforehand of the mighty results which would come to mankind from the birth of their children. There had always been to my mind, as to every Christian child's, a charm over the birth of the Saviour ; more tender and touching than over the birth of any other of all the countless myriads of babes that have ever opened their eyes to the light or the sorrows of earth. And what celestial anthems ever greeted a child's coming ? And suddenly there was with

the angel a multitude of the heavenly host, prais-
ing God and saying, " Glory to God in the highest
and on earth peace, good will toward men."

The Transfiguration of Christ next arrested my
attention.   Taking three of his disciples with him
into a mountain he showed to them his spiritual
body in all its brightness and glory, and with
him also appeared Moses and Elijah, and talked
with him of his approaching decease at Jerusalem.
The disciples saw all this ; they heard the language, they comprehended the whole scene, and
they remembered it and left a clear account of it
afterward.

I had often heard all these spiritual communications and angelic apparitions classed among *the
miracles*, and they said that the angels were
another order of beings, different from mortals
or departed earth's inhabitants.   But I found that
some of the most notable and glorious of them,
Samuel, Moses, and Elijah, were the most illustrious characters in Jewish history.   And further
on I saw that at the time of the crucifixion many
of those who were dead went into the Holy City
and appeared unto the living, as Christ himself

did to his disciples on several occasions, eating and drinking with them after he rose from the dead. So, too, he was seen by upward of five hundred persons at once when he went away into heaven. I found also that all these things were not only accepted as facts by all the early Christians, but that Christianity and its whole system of faith and worship rested on this foundation alone. It always has rested there, and it rests there to day. Hence I concluded, as I thought every impartial reader would, that these plain facts being universally accepted, there was no diversity in belief of *continued existence of each soul in a spiritual body after death—of their return from the spirit world to communicate with mortals, and the certainty of immortal life.*

Here for a time at least I was content to rest. I could now repose on what seemed to me solid ground. I had always, like all intelligent children, been drawn irresistibly to the story of the life and deeds of Jesus of Nazareth, and often wept over all he suffered in his blessed mission to save his fellow-men. I no longer allowed the dark and dismal sectarian theology in which I had been brought up to cloud every thought of life or death. In the exalted teachings and pure life of Jesus, and in his revelation and demonstration of immortality, I found enough to satisfy all my longings for a knowledge of an endless life to come. As He had interpreted God, I found a Father in Heaven.

IV.

THE SPIRITUALISM OF THE GREEKS.

I HAD reached satisfactory conclusions on the subject of spiritualism as preserved in the Jewish writings of the Old and New Testaments, and I then proposed to follow up the investigation of the evidence of the same belief among the ancient Greeks.

Here I had no reluctance to overcome, for the classics had made us familiar with the entire literature of the spiritual beings whose myriad forms breathed life and light through the vast realm of mythology, and those spiritual beings seemed nearer and more real than the mysterious, far-off angels of the stern old Hebrew days. The celestial forms of the goddesses, nymphs, and graces were robed in more fascinating beauty, and their presence distilled the aroma of the warmest sympathy with the denizens of the earth.

To blind old Homer's spiritual eyes were opened the Olympian palaces of the gods, and he brought their innumerable hosts down to fix their homes among the dwellings of men from whom they sprang. Jove's delight was, like Jehovah's, " with the sons of men." In his dream Jacob saw a ladder stretching from earth to heaven, with clusters of angels continually passing either way. In Homer's vision heaven and earth were brought nearer together, and their intercourse never ceased. There was not a home without its worshipped divinity or its protecting spirit. Every grove, fountain, mountain, valley, river, bird, beast, or flower was carefully watched over by its protecting patron. Temples were everywhere erected to them, incense and sacrifices smoked on their altars. Socrates had his guardian spirit that never left him, and the fates of men and nations were revealed through mortal lips at the sacred shrine of Delphos. The Gods never turned a deaf ear to the implorations of their devout worshippers. Greece held no atheist, and a blasphemer was put to death.

Heaven's own inspiration breathed from the burning lips of Sappho, and guided the chisel of Phidias. It woke the thunders of Demosthenes and the deathless strains of Pindar. All Greece was a temple of spiritualism, and all Greeks were spiritualists.

V.

MY FIRST EXPERIENCE IN SPIRITUALISM.

I HAD now completed my careful investigation of the historic evidence of the truth of spirit intercourse between mortals and immortals, so far as it is alleged to have existed in ancient times.

I have given but a partial account of the authorities I examined, for my studies were by no means limited to the writings of the Jews and the Greeks. They embraced the wide field of what is considered authentic history, from the curious and astounding revelations by modern archæologists into the monuments of Egypt and the Asiatic nations, as well as the light thrown on these subjects by modern travellers.

I had pursued these studies with the sole purpose of tracing the history of men's belief in spiritualism, in the sense I use that word in this work. It ended in establishing my unwavering conviction that, so far as the record goes, spiritualism is the foundation of all the religious beliefs in all the ages, and that the return of the dead is the only demonstration of the truth of continued existence of mortals in life to come.

In the very nature of the case it could not be established as a *fact* on any other testimony or in any other way. As the problem was fully solved in my own mind by the records of antiquity, my next inquiry related to modern times, and I continued my investigations under the clearer and fuller light of succeeding centuries down to the present age, when the judgment of the most learned and impartial *savants* of all enlightened nations have laid the question to rest.

But I was determined to go still farther, and learn the truth by *personal experience*, and thus remove it from the field of *belief* into the realm of *knowledge*. This was the last step in rational and philosophical investigation, and how I took it I propose to relate with what candor, clearness, and impartiality I can command.

I had recently lost a beloved husband, whom

I regarded as one of the noblest of men, and in whose sudden departure I had experienced the sorest bereavement which a woman's heart is ever called on to suffer. In the depth of my sorrow I sent for an old friend of our family, whose name had long been a household word by our fireside— a gentleman whom my husband had intimately known and admired as a man of genius and culture, and whom he loved with an affection which he could hardly have cherished for any other man.

As our interview went on, I suddenly exclaimed in the agony of my grief:

"O my friend, how gladly would I exchange all my husband left me, and be poor and struggle for a living, if I could only converse with him, and see him again, and hear his voice before I go to meet him ? I often heard you and my husband speak of these things. Do you really *believe* we can hold actual conversation with our departed friends ? "

" No, it has long since ceased with me to be a matter of *belief.* I *know* that spiritualism is true. I *believe* multitudes of statements put forth on this

subject in every part of the world, for they ac-
cord very much with my own experience ; but
what I have seen and felt in my long experience
I *know*, and I know it to be true as absolutely,
and for the same reasons as I know any other
facts in my life."

"Tell me, then, do you think *I* can know it
too ? "

"I have every reason to suppose you can.
Millions of others have found it so, why should
not you ? "

"How ? " I asked ; "what must I do ? "

"Nothing but as a perfect stranger go with
me to a medium whom I have known and had
every reason to trust and respect, and saying not
a word to explain your object, wait and see what
will come. You need not even have any plan ;
but wait till you get there, and then think and
wish what you please. Choose your day and
hour, and I will notify him by a postal-card. In
this way there can be no collusion, for he will
only get the notice. I shall say nothing more,
nor will you."

"That seems all best."

" Now name the time."

" This is Friday," I said ; " make it Sunday at eleven."

" I will."

The postal was despatched. At the hour my friend called, and with two lady acquaintances we drove to Mr. James V. Mansfield's residence and were seated. The gentleman entered, and he received us courteously and asked if we wanted a *séance*. He requesting that only one of the party should enter his *séance*-room at a time, I entered, when the folding-doors were closed. It was a beautiful sunny front room on the corner of Fifty-sixth Street and Sixth Avenue, on all sides of which hung portraits and landscapes, while in every nook and by-place, stood glass cabinets, which contained all sorts of books and relics and curiosities, which had been given or sent to him from friends and strangers from every part of the world. Their history I only learned afterward. My business alone on which I had gone was uppermost in my mind. I spoke to ask him what I should do.

" Nothing, madam, but to sit at that little table in the corner there and take a slip of paper and write any request you please to any departed friend whom you desire to hear from, and fold it and seal it as closely as you please. I will retire to this side room and come in, and we will see what comes. I cannot tell you till it is received. I promise nothing."

He laid his hand on my folded and securely pasted scrawl, which contained several names of departed friends I wished to hear from.

Very soon Mr. Mansfield began to throw off to me as I sat near him, written communications purporting to come mostly from persons I had called for, as well as from others I had not thought of for years long gone by.

I was surprised, startled, amazed, and delighted. I recognized the handwriting of some throughout the entire communications; of others only the signatures; and in others still I recognized nothing till afterward. But in most of them I saw at a flash unmistakable proof of the authorship and presence of the chief and dearest friends whom my heart longed most earnestly to hear from.

Besides all this, these messages were no common or indefinite greetings, which might have suited almost any occasion, but they were sharp and special statements, which fitted in closely to facts in my own life which could only have been known to myself and the persons sending the messages. They were not, moreover, limited to past occurrences ; but they embraced an intimate knowledge of occupations and designs known to no mortals but myself, for they had not passed my lips.

I will try not to weary the reader by recounting any considerable portion of the communications I received through Mr. Mansfield, although they would show a record of facts which put it entirely out of my power to doubt the authenticity of their origin. They concerned too many persons, and enumerated too many incidents in my life which had faded from my memory until they were sharply recalled.

Many visitors came whom I had neither called for nor thought of for years ; too many test questions, which I asked, were accurately responded to by the only individuals who could have answered them ; too many inquiries which I put

only, *mentally* were too quickly and clearly answered, and in every instance in plain writing
which the medium handed to me over the table,
while no word passed between us—that to doubt
the genuineness and truth of the whole thing,
would have been as impossible as to have questioned my own existence in any other scenes of life.

This first *séance* settled my conviction of the
reality and truth of the intercourse of beings in the
flesh with the departed, and I could, as a reasoning mind, as easily have rejected it as I could have
rejected the evidence of the death of my husband, or the birth of my only son.

All these records I took away with me and I
preserve them still. On scanning them critically,
there were some which I could not make out at
first, for though they were legibly enough written, I could not recall circumstances nor signatures, or I could not remember the incidents.
But gradually they came back to me one by one,
and I felt ashamed that I had allowed cherished
names and tender associations, once so dear, to
fade from my memory. I made it up to them
afterward, and I shall never forget them again !

This intercourse, and above all this actual and practical communion with my dead friends, seemed too precious to be true. It was too good, too grand, too real to my soul to be actually so !

I looked it all over. I scanned every word. I went so far as to search through my private *escritoire*, where I had preserved my most precious letters and written *memoria*, and I found such confirmations that I felt it would have been cruel not to have accepted them as facts, had they been living.

Could I go further, and not have done violence to my very being? I sat alone and thought ! "No," I answered; "it is true, or nothing is true."

I can never tell to another how much comfort came to my soul when I reached the full conviction that I had at last found substantial proof of the great fact—that I had solved the delightful problem of the possibility of the living conversing familiarly with the departed.

I felt now that I was standing on solid ground, as firm as the solid floor on which I stood. There could be no better proof than what I had. It was enough for me; all I could ask.

I reposed peacefully. If I tried at my best I could hardly give a more truthful or accurate an idea of my convictions or feelings than I have given in this simple recital. Nor can I find words to express the higher feeling that filled my soul, when I went to my pillow that brightest night of my life.

But I did not end here; for happy as I was in thus moving into, to me, an unexplored land, I did not feel like an intruder, least of all like a stranger. It was a surprise, and even a succession of surprises. It was a wandering along the open scenery of a clear stream which in its meanderings beguiled me through its gentle passages to the far-off sea.

It was more than peaceful—more than delicious —that sweet word which sums up so much that conveys what is pleasant to us. It was a new and a brighter outlook on to a summer land where I could almost see the homes of our loved ones as they dwell there, and with a sharpness of delineation which could define that scenery with accuracy, even to the dwellers of that sphere themselves.

And yet it seemed to me that I could and should go *farther*. Something said to me : " Go on, for we can and will come *nearer* to you, and prove to you by undoubted *physical proofs* that we are immortal, as you will be. "

VI.

HOW I SAW THE IMMORTALS.

I NOW leave for a time what may seem to trench on the improbable and perhaps on the more marvellous still. But to a vast multitude who are now living, and to the innumerable who people the spirit realms, it will not be considered as any nearer to the full reality, than the shadow which indicates the presence of truth. But *they* will understand it as truth.

Having arrived at this point of conviction—as I have described my progress, I wished to go still further. I feared I may have been guilty of temerity, but I could not repress the desire to witness positive evidence of *the personal appearance of some of my departed friends, who should actually prove to me their presence in person, as plainly and*

*convincingly as they did while they were living ;
and even in my own home.*

I had read of such appearances, and wished to
get such a crowning proof of their real presence,
as would entirely satisfy me. I knew I had had
proofs enough of my intercourse with their minds
and souls ; but I longed to see themselves *unmis-
takably.*

I had also longed (perhaps unreasonably) for
such an exhibition so earnestly that I felt it would
some day come. I could not think it unreason-
able to expect it.   I had no idea that anything
wonderful, least of all anything miraculous, would
happen to me.   But I had become so convinced
with a consciousness of the intercourse between
mortals and the immortals, that it appeared only
natural that some, at least, of my loved ones,
should come to me, so real, that I could not but
open my arms and embrace them.

And at last, the door opened visibly to me, between the two worlds. Plain enough to several
spectators, but not quite enough for me. I must
wait, and I was not impatient, for I really believed
my time would come. During this interval, I felt

a peaceful composure, and even a more complete serenity of mind than I had felt for a long time.

I went to my usual occupations at home, and attended to my many, and somewhat important engagements outside, with as much precision as ever ; only with a cheerfulness which was so new to me after the sore troubles through which I had passed. The dawn of a new day seemed to be breaking.

VII.

HOW AND WHEN I SAW DEPARTED FRIENDS.

ON my arrival in New York from Paris, an old friend, well known in Spiritualist circles, Mr. John L. O'Sullivan, called on me. Knowing him to be a Spiritualist, I at once broached the subject and told him of my own experience. He said :

" Then so far you have never seen any of the materializing side of Spiritualism ? "

" No," I said, " nor do I know anything about it. Do, please, explain the nature of it to me."

" I can do better than that. I can take you to a materializing medium. When can you go ? "

" Ah ! when can you take me ? That is the only question."

" Let me see," said he. " This is Friday ; why, to-morrow night, Saturday night, I will call for you and your friend, Mrs. Swift " (the lady who accompanied me from Paris). "To-morrow night at half-past seven ; *séance* at eight."

Punctual to the hour he arrived; and we three started for Mrs. Williams' home in Thirty-fourth Street. On the way, I mentioned to Mr. O'Sullivan that I preferred he should not introduce me, or mention my name, as I was investigating, and wished to give myself full opportunity to test it. (They did not know me for two months afterward.)

We arrived at the house five minutes before eight, and were ushered into the *séance*-room, where some fifteen persons were seated. The room was gas lighted, sufficiently to read by. Shortly after the medium entered, and said : " Friends, I presume you have come here to see and hear from your friends. It depends entirely upon yourselves what you may receive. If you give them good conditions, you will have good results."

She then entered the cabinet, and that was the last seen of her that night by us. The room was an ordinary sized parlor, with a cabinet at one corner with a curtain drawn across, some seven feet high, and open at the top.

The medium invited friends to examine the cabinet before she entered it.   Two strange gentlemen examined it, and pronounced it in all respects to their satisfaction.   After the medium entered the cabinet, the gentleman who sat at a piano requested those present to join in singing "Nearer, my God, to Thee."

After perhaps five minutes, the curtain opened and I, for the first time, saw what purported to be a spirit—a beautiful person.   The lady who conducted the cabinet said: "This is Priscilla, one of the guides of the medium, who comes to bless the circle."

After a few seconds she closed the curtain, and singing was resumed.

Further along in this book, I shall explain who Priscilla is, as I subsequently learned.   Next, the curtain opened, and a gentleman in citizen's dress appeared.   The lady who conducted the *séance* said: "This is Mr. Prentice Holland, another guide of the medium, who remains in the cabinet to answer questions of a spiritual nature, that any one in the audience may wish to ask.   Also, if the friends wish to go to the cabinet and address him, he will be very happy to answer any question they desire to put to him." He addressed some questions, and two or three gentlemen went up and had quite prolonged conversation with him.

The next spirit that appeared was one about sixteen years of age, who opened the curtain, throwing his arms out from it, and with a very boyish voice said: "Mamma! oh, Mamma!" He was instantly responded to by a lady in the audience who went up to the curtain, saying:

"Oh, is that you, darling?"

He threw his arms around her neck, kissed her on the cheek, loud enough for any one in the room to hear. Then he dematerialized and disappeared.

The lady turned to the audience and said:

"This is my son; thank God he has been able to return to me."

Next, a young lady came and beckoned to a gentleman in the audience, calling him to her. Taking his arm and walking about, she put her hand in his coat pocket, and took out a letter, then put it back again, and whispering something to him, disappeared behind the curtain.

4

Several other figures appeared, and were recognized by their friends.

Then a gentleman came and beckoned to Mr. O'Sullivan, who went to the curtain where he held a conversation. Returning he said that was Mayor Wood. Of course I did not recognize him, never having seen him.

There must have appeared that night eighteen or twenty figures, all recognized by some of their friends.

But none of *my* friends came to me during that *séance;* and, I must say, I felt somewhat disappointed. But as it was my first experiment, I had no right to expect anything.

Mr. O'Sullivan said : " You must go two or three times, and I am sure you will be rewarded for your trouble by finding some of your dear ones come to you."

"Well," I said, " I will see." But my mind was then very much confused.

He said, " I hope you are not disappointed."

" Oh, no," I replied ; " I am not disappointed. I shall give this a thorough trial, and, perhaps, a few weeks hence I may be able to talk more about it to you. At present, I do not sufficiently understand it to give you what I would consider a definite answer."

The following morning, Sunday, I got ready as usual about ten o'clock, not knowing whether I would go to church, or take a walk. But Mrs. Swift and myself sauntered out about the time the church bells were ringing. Finding ourselves on Thirty-fourth Street, I said :

" This is near where the medium lives. Suppose, instead of going to church, we just go in here and see her ; perhaps I can learn something."

We found ourselves in Mrs. Williams' reception room, and in a moment the lady entered herself. I must say I was very much impressed with her appearance and conversation, in contrast with the tricks, trap-doors, and other surroundings that some mediums are said to have about them. I felt that she bore the stamp of truth in looks and conversation. I never mentioned that I had been there the night before. She did not know my name, nor that of my friend, nor anything about us. Then I said :

" Mrs. Williams, can you give us a private *séance* to-morrow morning ? "

She said : " Let us see ; what engagement have I for to-morrow morning ? " The lady who admitted us, immediately answered : " None that I know of." Then she said : " You can have a *séance* at eleven o'clock." I thanked her and left.

Punctual to the hour next morning, my friend and I entered the *séance* room of Mrs. Williams ; only Mrs. Swift and myself were in the room. The doors were locked, and the medium, looking at me, said :

" You are a stranger ; it is my custom to invite strangers to examine my cabinet. Have you any desire to do so ? "

For a moment I felt that it would be an outrage to enter her cabinet for that purpose. But then, in order to satisfy a friend to whom I might mention it, I thought I would examine it. But I said : " I have no doubt about it myself." So my friend and I went into the cabinet. We found a solid wall on one side by a window which was boarded up, the front opening into the room ; carpet on the floor, and solid under our feet. There could be no possible way in which anybody could get access to that cabinet save from the front where we sat.

"Now," I said to myself, "if anything comes through this cabinet, it will have to be through spiritual agency, for no mortal can :" of that I was satisfied.

After we were seated there some three or four minutes, a little childish voice proceeded from the cabinet and said :

"Good morning, Mrs. Swift ; good morning, Mrs. Kate." This somewhat startled me. I looked at Mrs. Swift and said :

"Good gracious! how did she know our names?" She laid her hand upon me and said :

"Listen! she is talking." The spirit continued :

"Mrs. Swift, how did you leave everybody in Paris? You remember the dear Count B—— ?"

This somewhat surprised Mrs. Swift, as she was very sure that nobody knew anything about their affairs in Paris, or of the many *séances* they had had with the Count. I subsequently learned that the voice was that of little " Bright Eyes," the dear little Mexican girl, and one of the guides of the medium.

A few moments elapsed when my friend exclaimed, "Oh, John!" Attention was drawn to the curtain.

I turned my eyes toward the curtain, and there stood the figure of a man arrayed in purest white, with a black beard descending to his breast, falling half a yard or more in length.

" Amie, my child," said he. I was surprised. I had never heard Mrs. Swift called by that name before. I subsequently learned that it was a pet name that John King had given Mrs. Swift in Paris during their many *séances.* They spoke together for some time, and then Mrs. Swift said :

" Come with me." And I walked to the cabinet, and stood in the presence of the first materialized spirit I had ever spoken with. I seemed to have lost all fear, and spoke to the spirit, and looked at him as though I had been accustomed to talk with spirits, and see them all my life.

He said to me: " My child, I thank you for your many kindnesses to my friend."

I knew instantly to whom he referred—a friend who frequently attended *séances* with Mrs. Swift in Paris to whom I had rendered kindnesses. But, I must say, I was surprised. However, all such things cease to be a wonder, now that I so well understand spirit matters.

Mrs. Swift, in all that *séance*, had five different spirits come to her, with all of whom she had been familiar in Paris.

She recognized them all, had long conversations with them, and they seemed to be as familiar with her as I was, who had known her fifteen years.

As yet I had none come to me, and I confess that I had begun to feel that perhaps I was forgotten, when the curtain opened and a beautiful figure in white said :

" Katy, this is Hattie ! "

I knew this spirit—knew the figure. It was that of my sister—my dear sister who had passed away some six years before. I was soon at the curtain conversing with her. She there and then said so many things that none but she and I could possibly have known, and spoken about, that I was at once convinced from her language, if from nothing else, that it was my sister, Harriet. She spoke of my husband, and said : " He is here ; he is speaking to you. Oh, do try and hear him."

But my ears were too dull. I heard nothing but her voice. This was all the spirit friend, that came to me that forenoon. But I was firmly convinced that there was no deceit ; that what we saw were really spirits, and I fully determined, then and there, to investigate it to the end of the letter.

This was the first of the many *séances* that I have had since, the results of which I intend to give further along.

VIII.

AS I WENT ON.

HAVING become somewhat familiar in two *séances* with the "phenomena," as they call them, I thought I would try another public *séance*, and see how they proceeded, so that I might compare my private with the public ones.

At the next *séance* sat a lady whom I at once recognized, from her manner and language, as coming from Ireland. After the *séance* commenced "Bright Eyes" addressed her by her name, and said:

"Dear lady, your little daughter is here tonight."

The lady asked: "Will she come to me?"

"Why, certainly! most assuredly. That is what you are here for—to see her."

A gentleman asked her: "Dear Bright Eyes, what is my name and where did I come from?"

"Well," said she, in a very factious way, "it is a pity you don't know your own name, or where you came from. Perhaps we will find out by and by." Later on she said:

" Mr. ——, of such a place, I shall visit you at your hotel, and open your ears."

He said: " You have really found out my name; how did you do it?"

" Why, by your mother giving me your full name. And your sister is here. They are all telling about your little peculiarities. They know them as well as you do yourself."

Now to return to the little Irish lady whose daughter was announced from the cabinet.

The curtain opened and a girl about sixteen years of age with jet black hair, rushing across the floor, put out her arms and said:

" Oh! dear mother." In a moment they were in each other's arms and sobbing like two children. It touched us all so much there was not a dry eye in the whole audience. A more affecting scene I never witnessed. The mother said:

"Oh! thank God! thank God! that he has permitted me to live to see my child."

"Friends," she said, "this little girl passed away when she was twelve years of age, at a Convent School in Ireland."

Next appeared the brother of a gentleman in the audience, who had been a naval officer in our late war. He came in his full uniform, cap, buttons and all. The likeness between himself and the Doctor, his brother, was so striking that several noticed it, and spoke of it, when the Doctor said:

"Oh, yes, but I am a little the better looking of the two!"

"No," some one said; "Captain Fred is the best looking."

The Doctor at once walked up to the curtain, the Captain drew it aside, and stood facing the audience in full gas-light. The Captain touched his cap and said: "Friends, I was Frederick G. S—— in what you call life—for there is no such thing as death."

Next came "Crowfoot," another guide of the medium; the man who, in life, must have weighed

nearly three hundred pounds.   He stood six feet
four; while the medium was certainly rather an
undersized lady, and by no possible means could
she have elongated herself to be of the size of
Crowfoot.   He spoke to the audience and said:

"Me come to bless and give strength.   If anybody in the audience wish to go up and speak
to Crowfoot they can do so.   He is always very
glad to talk to the Squaws, and the Braves."

Nobody seemed inclined to go, but Crowfoot
selected a lady from the audience who had a
severe cough.   He said, "Me want to relieve the
sick."   He said, "No fear of me."   She turned
her back, and he rubbed it six or seven seconds.
It gave her a great deal of pleasure.   She thanked
him and returned to her seat.   He said to her:

"You all right now.   Now squaw you all right."

Next appeared Carrie Miller, the daughter of
Mr. Miller (editor of the *Psychometric Circular* of
Brooklyn).   She walked to the middle of the floor,
called up two gentlemen, friends of her father's,
gave them messages, and the spirit in a few seconds dematerialized outside of the curtain.

"There!" said a gentleman who sat behind me.

"I came all the way from Canada to see this. It is my first appearance at any materializing circle; but, after seeing what I have this night, I am not at all sorry I came, and I only wish that all the clergymen and Christians of my place could see what I have seen. Why, that young lady disappeared into nothing."

So every one felt, for we all saw it in plain light, and we could not all have been enchanted, deluded, or deceived.

IX.

A DARK SÉANCE.

THE next *séance* was to be a dark one. I received an invitation from Mrs. Williams to join a few friends in a dark circle at her house. This was another and to me a new phase in spirit manifestations. I had never been in a dark circle, and could not really say, even to myself, how it would affect me. However, Mrs. Swift and myself arrived and found two or three intimate friends of the medium's awaiting us, say five in all.

We entered the *séance* room, and Mrs. Williams retired to her cabinet. The doors were all locked, the lights turned out, and joining hands we awaited the result.

Some four or five minutes elapsed, when the voice of Mr. Holland greeted us with—

" Good evening, children ; I am glad to meet you all."

I sat at the end of the company next to the wall. I must say it was a novel experience to me, to be in the dark, waiting, for what the world terms, " ghost manifestations." While I was thinking of the novelty of my situation, I felt a hand on my shoulder, and a voice whispered in my ear :

" I am here, darling."

It was the voice of my husband, and I knew it. He stood by my side, with my hand in his for about fifteen minutes, conversing on affairs connected with our family. The night was very warm and I had a pocket-handkerchief with which I dried the perspiration on my forehead. My husband took the handkerchief out of my hand, wiped my forehead with it, arranged my hair, and passed the handkerchief back to me. I took it out of his hand ; and, as I did so, his hand rested in mine. I held it a few seconds, and then after a time he was gone.

All around me I heard spirit voices, and I saw white spirit lights passing before me. The next moment my mother's name appeared in illuminated letters in front of me. Simultaneously my friends saw illuminated names passing in front of them.

I think that night more than ten different spirit friends spoke to me. They seemed to have much more strength in a dark circle than in a light one. They could remain longer. Little " Bright Eyes " came out, sat by my side, took hold of my dress, and kissed me on the cheek, saying :

" Miss Katy, do you know whose voice this is speaking to you ? "

I answered : " I know you are Little ' Bright Eyes.' "

That same night while singing " Nearer, my God, to Thee " she joined in, and we could hear her voice distinctly.

To me, this dark *séance* was even more marvellous than a light one. Four or five spirits were talking at the same time, and as we all held hands, and the medium was sound asleep, or entranced in the cabinet, and no mortal could have entered the room, I went home that night more fully convinced of the truth of spiritual intercourse than in all my previous experiences.

X.

A PRIVATE SÉANCE.

MY next *séance* was a private one.   There were only four of us ; Prof. J. Jay Watson being one of the number.   He had travelled all over Europe with Ole Bull, and been his companion for some years.   He had also received from him the very violin which he held in his hand that night, playing a favorite piece which he had dedicated to Ole Bull's daughter in Sweden.   When the curtain opened, there stood Ole Bull himself, as natural as in life.   His long hair was pushed back from his forehead, his shirt ruffled as he used to wear it, and, in every way, he appeared the perfect reflex of Ole Bull, as I had seen him.   He looked toward the professor and said :

" Votson ! Votson ! Votson ! "—three times.

5

He need not have uttered it but once; for the professor has a very fine ear, and knew the voice instantly. They laughed and talked together in the Norwegian tongue I supposed, for at least ten minutes, one voice being as perfectly distinct as the other. When the professor took his seat, Ole Bull bowed to us all, said a few pleasant words, and disappeared from our sight.

I would here say, that, during life, Ole Bull was a confirmed Spiritualist, and was convinced that his wonderful musical talent was aided by spirit influence, and that he was often inspired to play the beautiful strains that had so charmed his audiences. Professor Watson had not been a Spiritualist, and could scarcely understand Ole Bull when he told him sometimes of these strange things. But he confesses, that he can now understand more fully what was told him then, than he ever expected to be able to, for, not being a Spiritualist, he could not enter into the matter as Ole Bull did, nor comprehend the theory of it.

My mother-in-law then came. She was a very advanced spirit, with strong vocal organs as in life. She addressed us, saying : " Children, the day is not far distant when, if you give us the proper conditions, we shall be able to appear on the rostrum in bright daylight, and talk to you as I am doing now."

XI.

OLE BULL, THE GREAT NORWEGIAN VIOLIN-IST, AS A SPIRITUALIST.

LEARNING from Professor J. Jay Watson, the well-known American violinist spoken of in this *séance*, that he was a life-long and intimate friend of Ole Bull, I ventured to ask him to favor me with some account of the great Norwegian's alleged belief in Spiritualism, and he kindly favored me with the following relation, which will doubtless prove interesting to the reader :

RESPECTED FRIEND : Your esteemed favor is at hand, and I most cheerfully comply with your request to give you a few incidents connected with the life of the late Ole Bull, especially those bearing upon his belief as a Spiritualist. In all his marvellous performances he was aided and influenced by spirit power. Mozart was his " beau ideal " as a musician, and the immortal works of that inspired master he considered sacredly beautiful. In rendering the music of Mozart, his reverence for this great composer revealed itself in his performances, and invariably produced a deep impression on his hearers. Those who have made the master-pieces of Mozart the study of a lifetime, who have edited his works and dwelt upon the perfection of their instrumentation, have also said that Ole Bull's interpretation of those, especially of the *adagios*, showed a deeper and more appreciative understanding of their author's intention than had ever before been attained by any other master. Ole Bull used to say that "Mozart was his religion." To him there could be no more beautiful, no loftier expression of human thought and aspirations than he found in the works of this transcendent genius. He once remarked to me that the spirit of Mozart had been by his side constantly when he was playing the violin since his twenty-fourth year.

I will here add that it was about this time that Ole Bull composed his famous " Mother's Prayer," which has touched many a mother's heart, and is probably the most widely known solo ever performed upon the violin. In speaking to me of this charming inspiration, he said, " I composed it because I could not help it."

His love for the genius of Mozart was displayed in a most tangible manner at Salsburg, the home of Mozart. It was in Salsburg that Ole Bull proposed and gave the first grand concert for the " Mozart Fund," having at this same concert the supreme satisfaction of seeing Mozart's widow among his auditors.

In the city of Bergen, in Norway, on February 5, 1810, Ole Bull first saw the light. On the picturesque " Lysö "

("Island of Light"), a short distance from Bergen, is situated the home of Ole Bull, which he built a few years previous to his demise. From the music-room of this delightful retreat the soul of the genial musician took its flight on August 18, 1880. As his spirit was passing away to the beautiful "Land o' the Leal," he requested a lady friend who was present to perform upon the organ Mozart's immortal "Requiem." This, his last wish, so touchingly beautiful and suggestive, was promptly gratified.

Ole Bull's first visit to America was in 1843, his second in 1852, and his third visit was made in 1867 at my earnest request, through a letter which I wrote him while he was sojourning in Paris. Immediately upon the reception of my letter he made a hasty preparation and departed for America. Upon his arrival in New York he called upon me and greeted me with a genuine Norwegian hug, at the same time exclaiming, in his quaint broken English, " My dear Vatsohn, dot ish de hug of a Norwegian bear ; " to which I replied, " I should call it the hug of a Norwegian Bull." He laughingly exclaimed " Bravo ! " and immediately alluding to my letter he said, " It was that which has brought me again to America ; and," continued he, " I thank you very much indeed for the kind invitation. It came at a very auspicious moment." He then proposed playing gratuitously for my friends and pupils at my musical institution. His generous offer was of course accepted. At this entertainment were many prominent persons, among whom might be mentioned Major-General Robert Anderson, the hero of Fort Sumter ; Col. Rush C. Hawkins, of the famous " Hawkins' Zouaves ; " Andrew J. Graham, the author of " Standard Phonography ; " Dr. O. R. Gross, and Mrs. Leah Underhill, the eldest of the celebrated Fox sisters, through whose mediumship the marvellous " Rochester rappings" had attracted the attention of the whole civilized world. Ole Bull and myself performed, alternately, several pieces upon the violin, assisted by Miss Annie A. Watson, the pianiste. During the music loud raps were constantly being heard in different parts of the parlor. As there was not more than one hundred persons present, and their attention being principally occupied with the music and conversation, it is doubtful if many, except a few who understood the phenomena, noticed the raps. The demonstrations, however, of spirit power continuing to increase, Mrs. Underhill decided to retire from the parlor, when in a short time the rapping ceased entirely.

A few evenings subsequent to this episode, this lady was kind enough to give Ole Bull and myself a sitting at her private residence. Although she had long before this ceased to act as a public medium, the experiences of this evening were very remarkable and highly satisfactory, the mediumistic powers of Mrs. Underhill still being as marvellous as they ever were. On another occasion, at her house, my little son Emmons H. Watson, a lad at that time about eight years of age, while quietly sitting in a chair, was moved by some unseen power, giving great delight to the little fellow as he gently glided over the floor, until he came in contact with a large dining-table at which some half dozen or more persons were sitting. " Papa, I wish it would do so some more," he exclaimed in high glee. All present witnessed this wonderful manifestation, the room being fully lighted at the time. I will here add that it was in this very room that the Hon. Robert Dale Owen pursued his spiritual investigations while gathering material for one of his late works on Spiritualism. Dr. J. V. Mansfield and Mr. Charles H. Foster were the mediums whom Ole Bull most frequently visited. One evening a party of five, consisting of Ole Bull, his son Alexander Bull, Prof. Vincenzo B—— (a distinguished scientist of this city and formerly a member of the Italian Parliament), the Professor's wife, and myself, visited Mr. Foster for the purpose of witnessing his marvellous powers as a medium. Ole Bull and his son received many remarkable tests, causing the latter to almost lose his self-control. Suddenly turning to Prof. B—— Mr. Foster said: " There is a lady spirit present who tells me she is an aunt of yours; she carries in her hand a beautiful flower which she calls *Margarita.*" Prof. B—— made no reply. Mr. Foster continued : " The lady tells me also that her name is *Margarita,* and that she was born and passed away in the village of Margarita." These three wonderful tests seemed to stagger the learned professor as he immediately confirmed *facts* which he said were known only to himself. Said the professor: " I had an aunt by the name of Margarita who passed away in Italy in a little village called Margarita. This village is little known even among the Italian people, for it is situated in a mountainous district far away from the busy world. My aunt was very fond of the Italian daisy, which in the Italian language is called ' Margarita.' "

Several days after this remarkable experience I chanced to step into a Broadway stage in which Prof. B—— was a passenger. Our conversation soon turned upon the events experienced at Mr. Foster's rooms, and I took occasion to review the incidents connected with the wondrous tests. Prof. B—— confirmed his previous remarks, simply adding that "it was an occult force the cause of which he considered incomprehensible, and as yet unexplained by any scientific research."

Ole Bull emphatically pronounced himself a Spiritualist. Several of his friends and admirers, myself among the number, in response to an invitation of the great artist, one afternoon assembled at his rooms in the Fifth Avenue Hotel. After he had played as he alone could play when inspired by the magnetism of a few congenial friends, the subject turned upon Spiritualism. Most of those present were of the opinion that all gifted musicians receive great aid from the spirit world. One person present, however, took occasion to ridicule the philosophy in terms which were neither forcible nor elegant. Ole Bull, still holding his loved violin, and apparently lost in deep thought, suddenly raised himself to his full height, his large gray eyes flashing with indignation, and exclaimed, in a tone of voice decidedly fortissimo : " Gentlemen, I am a Spiritualist!" I need scarcely add that the offending culprit made no further attempt to ridicule the beautiful truths of spirit return. All present seemed awed by the energetic manner in which the great artist had given vent to his sentiments in five well-chosen words.

An immense concourse of people had gathered one afternoon in Steinway Hall to listen to the delightful strains of Ole Bull's violin. The audience was composed largely of

ladies. Many noted persons were present, among whom
I noticed the Hon. Horace Greeley, Hon. E. H. Stough-
ton, Wenzel Kopta (the gifted violinist), several well-known
pianists of both sexes, with a liberal sprinkling of musicians
from the various city orchestras. As the lamented Gott-
schalk once remarked : " It was an audience well calculated
to inspire one's soul to its utmost depths." I had rarely
heard Ole Bull perform so wondrously as upon this occasion,
and in the language of another, " I was certainly impressed
that afternoon as no man ever impressed me before. It
was a most glorious sensation to sit in that audience and
feel that all were elevated to the same pitch with myself.
My impulse was to speak to every one as an intimate
friend; the most remote or proud I did not fear or de-
spise; in that element they were all accessible, nay, all
worth reaching." This surely was the highest testimony to
his great art and his great soul. At the close of the concert the ante-rooms were crowded with hosts of admirers,
anxious to congratulate the great master upon the success of the entertainment. Dr. O. R. Gross, himself a fine
musician, and a warm personal friend of Ole Bull, grasped
him warmly by the hand, at the same time remarking :
" My dear Ole Bull, there were many silent listeners
in your audience this afternoon whom you did not
see." " Oh, yes ! oh, yes ! I know that," he said, " I
know that ; but although I could not see them I could
feel them all the same, especially when I was playing
the ' Mother's Prayer ;' and you know, dear Doctor, I
think that there were many mothers in my audience to-
day." Then like a pleased child he skipped around the

room, telling the incident to all with whom he came in contact.

But I have already exceeded the limits which I had prescribed for my letter. I cannot close, however, without mentioning briefly the astonishing experiences which I have recently had in the *séance*-rooms of Mrs. M. E. Williams, of this city, undoubtedly the most wondrous medium of the present day. At the earnest request of several friends I took the famous old Cremona violin presented me by Ole Bull, and performed several evenings upon it in connection with my friend Dr. Gross, who presided at the organ. Lucie Bull, a daughter of Ole Bull by his first wife, a beautiful young lady who passed away several years since in Norway, materialized in plain sight of some twenty or more persons, took the violin from my hands, reverently kissed it, and returned it to me. On another occasion I was playing upon the guitar a piece which I had frequently played for Lucie during my first visit to her father at his home in Norway in 1868. Lucie again materialized, crossed the room from the cabinet to near the organ where I was sitting, and gently touched the strings of the guitar several times. This was again repeated upon another occasion, each time in the presence of not less than twenty persons. Ole Bull himself has twice materialized at Mrs. Williams' cabinet, talking familiarly to several old friends who were present, promising at some time in the near future to prove his identity by playing upon his old favorite violin. I am aware that to multitudes the idea of a world in which beings exist as spirits without these gross bodies strikes them as a fiction. This is mournful, but not wonderful ; for how can men who immerse themselves in the body and its interests, and cultivate no acquaintance with their own souls and spiritual powers, comprehend a higher spiritual life ?

There are multitudes who pronounce man a visionary who speaks distinctly and joyfully of his future being, and of the triumph of the mind over bodily decay. This skepticism as to things spiritual and celestial is as irrational and unphilosophical as it is degrading ; for we have more evidence that we have souls or spirits than that we have bodies. As Longfellow so beautifully says :

> " She is not dead, the child of our affection,
>   But gone up to that school
>   Where she no longer needs our poor protection,
>   And God himself doth rule."

Fraternally yours for truth, gratitude, and impartial justice,

JOHN JAY WATSON,
27 Union Square, New York City.

XII.

DURING the summer of 1883 the annual camp-meeting of Spiritualists was held at Lake Cassadagua, and I attended it and remained two weeks. It was the first gathering of the kind at which I had assisted.

My friend Mrs. Swift and I stopped at a new and yet unfinished hotel, kept by Mrs. Alden and family. Knowing several of the mediums who were coming, I asked to see their rooms.

"This," I was told, "was for Mr. Allen, the musical medium;" the next was for Mr. Watkins, the slate-writer; and further on was Mrs. Williams', of New York, the materializing medium.

Here I found the workmen putting up what they called "a cabinet," of plain pine boards, on one side of the room. I asked the foreman if he was a Spiritualist. "No, ma'am! By no means. We believe those people are all a crazy set. What do you suppose young Alden told me when he gave me the dimensions of this cabinet? He said that the medium would have forty or fifty spirits in there. Now the cabinet is only a single board's thickness, and right under it is the dining-room, and if she brings in there any spirits I want to see them, and we boys are coming, and they can't play any of their tricks on us."

I had examined the room, the floor, and the cabinet, and remarked: "I see no trap-doors, nor false doors, nor any chance for deception."

"No, ma'am; we know what we built. Yes, I want to see them come. If they can bring them into or out of this room, or this cabinet, I want them to bring out an old uncle of mine who died in California very rich, and I want to find out what became of his money."

"I am afraid, my dear man," I said, "if you come for money and not from love, you may be disappointed; for it is only love that brings our spirit friends."

"Ah! that's it, then!" and his expression of

incredulity was worth seeing. But he had something yet to learn.

HENRY ALLEN, THE MUSICAL MEDIUM.

That afternoon I made an appointment with Henry Allen, to see a temporary little structure for a display of his alleged musical mediumistic gifts. It was a small building put up by the side of the hotel, in the shape of a sugar-loaf, enclosed with single plain boards, and with no entrance except by a curtain suspended at the opening where ordinarily a door would be hung. Five of us friends entered. The curtain was securely closed, when we were asked by Mr. Allen to examine the room. In the centre was a little plain table and around it were twenty plain chairs. It was dark outside, but the room was fully lit up by two lamps, and we saw and examined five musical instruments lying together on the table, viz., *a violin*, *a guitar*, *a banjo*, *a zither*, and *a flute*.

We were seated and joined hands, I holding the medium's right hand and Mrs. Swift the left, when one of our party turned down the lamps, and we were left in perfect darkness. In this position, with joined hands, we sat during the whole time of the *séance*. Not one of the circle could have moved a hand without being instantly discovered.

When we became quiet, all the five instruments began to play in perfect harmony, first loud, and then gradually softer, till like music at a distance it became almost inaudible, when it returned as it had retreated, and at last sounded with its full power and ceased.

This display we all judged lasted about fifteen minutes, filling us with amazement and delight. Mr. Allen then said that if each one of us would in turn sit by his side, and hold his right hand and wish *mentally* to have some particular piece played by the spirit band, he believed it would be done.

Sitting as I still was on his right hand, I thought of a favorite Italian *aria*, not commonly known, and the band at once produced it in perfection. Each of my friends followed, one by one, and mentally indicated her desire, and with the same result, when we could not find words to express our surprise and admiration. Some if not all of us had voices, and ears long trained, and were as perfectly satisfied as we had ever been with any instrumental music in the whole course of our lives.

But the wonders of that evening were not yet to cease. Shortly after this the entire room seemed to be filled with spirits. My own friends came to me first, among them my own mother, who pressed her arms around my neck, and I laid my head on her shoulder and felt her caresses as tangibly as I ever did in her mortal life. This embrace and her loving words lasted many minutes. Then as many as twelve other departed friends followed in succession, each calling his or her name, and asking and answering questions and demonstrating their identity. Some of them had never visited me before as spirits, but all proved their presence beyond the possibility of doubt.

Then came the opportunity for each of my companions as she took her place by the medium's side and held his hand. They all had similar demonstrations made to them by their departed till nothing further seemed left for any one to de-

6

sire. When these affecting scenes closed, and we had all resumed our first seats, the music of the spirits began again, and a great number of other pieces were played with corresponding matchless harmony and effect.

As the music ceased, writing was heard, and each one had brought to and laid on our hands slips of paper, perfectly legible afterward in the light, one and all being messages of love from departed ones whose handwriting was clearly recognized. The parting strains were then played; our hands, which had not once been unclasped since they were first united, except for the instants when we had to change places, were now free; the lamps were lit; we saw all the five instruments laying on the table where we first saw them, and bidding the medium a tender goodnight retired to our rooms in the hotel. None of us attempted to describe the strange and overpowering feelings which these scenes had inspired, nor shall I.

I afterward attended five or six other public *séances* of Mr. Allen, all of which were as satisfactory and some of them even more wonderful than the first. Many parties from neighboring towns and villages, and others from distant places, attended these *séances;* but I heard no doubt expressed by any of them, whether Spiritualists or not, when they came, about the genuineness of the phenomena presented, nor their convincing power over every candid and impartial observer.

WATKINS, THE SLATE-WRITER.

This gentleman has the highest reputation, I believe, of any similarly gifted medium in the country.

This phase of alleged supermundane power had always possessed for me a curious interest, and although it seemed to belong to a lower plane than some others, I was inclined to class it among that vast range of wonderful gifts which have in all ages been displayed by certain individuals, whose exceptional endowments excited amazement rather than unbelief. Their *origin* was shrouded in mystery, but *the facts* were not denied; to all observers the phenomena were beyond dispute.

I have chosen the word *supermundane* rather

than *supernatural*, for I do not believe that anything exists within the boundless realm of the
created universe which can properly be called
supernatural.   That epithet can be correctly ap-
plied to the Creator alone.   This idea is what im-
parts to Humboldt's " Cosmos " and Job's sublime
Allegory their infinite charm.

In a universe of law there can be no miracle,
as that term is commonly defined to be a violation
of, or an exception to, law.   All things are mysteries till they are understood ; but the cosmos
admits no miracle but its own creation—no in-
solvable mystery but the existence of God—all
else is nature.

It seems to me, therefore, that in adopting the
word supra (or super) mundane, instead of super
(or supra) natural, a useful and even necessary
change is made, for it not only corrects a great
error, but removes the objection in many minds
to the reasonable reception of Spiritualism and its
philosophy.

If I were attempting to write a dissertation on
the philosophical basis of Spiritualism, instead of
giving an honest account of my spiritualistic ex-

perience and observation, I should appeal to my reader's consciousness and inquire if mortals who are too weak to prolong their lives here beyond their last breath, have not often involuntarily turned their thoughts to heaven for help which earth alone could not give ? That help which we all implore in moments of weakness or peril can only come from spiritual sources. That aspiration for strength which earth cannot give, is the foundation of all religious emotions, of all religions, and of all Spiritualism. These sentiments, emotions, and yearnings are all natural to man, and are inseparable from his existence as an immortal being.

But to come to our first *séance* with the slate-writer. He had arrived only the previous evening, but an engagement was secured for an interview the next morning. At 10 o'clock Mrs. Swift and myself called at his apartment in the hotel. After a courteous reception we glanced around the room, which showed nothing but the common furniture of a plain country hotel. After we were seated he handed to each of us a new double slate, with a damp sponge and a dry napkin.

"Now," he said, "keeping your seats, please. take twelve slips of that note-paper, and each write the names of twelve spirit friends, and crumple each one separately into a pellet, and then throw the whole twenty-four into a pile together so promiscuously on the table that neither of you could distinguish one from another."

He then turned his back on us and walked over to the window on the side of the room, and began talking with some one outside, and remained there till we told him our work was done. Then closing the window he returned to the table and requested us to point our pencils to, or with their points touch the pellets one by one deliberately. I began and carefully touched five in succession, and at the sixth the pencil suddenly was arrested by no will of my own.

"Now take up that pellet, madam, and hold it tight in one hand, and hand your slate to me with the other, and we will open and examine it closely, to see that there is no writing on either of the four sides. We need no pencil now." Closing the slate he held it over the table, and instantly we heard a scratching, and when the noise ceased he handed back the slate. I took it, and, as he requested, opened the pellet and read it. It contained only the words " Dear mother." Then opening the slate, I saw my mother's name clearly—and accurately spelled—written, which surprised me the more because of its being an unusual name which not one in a thousand, probably, who heard it pronounced would have spelled it correctly as she did.

The same process I continued with *my* remaining eleven pellets, taking up only those at which my pencil stopped, and not stopping at any other, while it was impossible for either my friend or myself to distinguish one from another, since the whole twenty-four had been made exactly alike, only that neither knew the names the other had written. The same process was strictly adhered to by us both until the little pile disappeared, and not the slightest mistake had been made even in the minutest point.

When these exercises were over, the medium passed under spirit control, and delivered to me a long message (Mrs. S. agreed with me that it could not have lasted less than twenty minutes)

in the voice and manner of my husband, as unmistakable to us both as though the whole had
occurred in our own home in years gone by when
we three often sat together. The demonstration
was greatly intensified to me because much of it
concerned my own personal affairs and circumstances which could not have been known to any
mortal on earth. I need hardly add that we left
Mr. Watkins with feelings of admiration for his
marvellous gifts, and of gratitude for his kind
ministrations which will never fade from our
memories.

XIII.

MRS. WILLIAMS' ARRIVAL AND FIRST PUBLIC SÉANCE.

ON the day following our visit to Mr. Watkins, Mrs. Williams arrived, and we assisted in unpacking her trunk and preparing her cabinet. It amused us very much to see the curiosity of the workmen when they were allowed to help in taking out the curtains, and to notice the blank expression on their faces at not finding any masks, wigs, or any of the usual paraphernalia which are supposed to make up the principal stock in trade of travelling actresses, female mediums, and mountebanks! They were evidently disappointed as they returned to resume their work.

That evening Mrs. W. held her first *séance*, which was attended by about twenty persons, most of whom had never witnessed a material-

ization, and nearly all being strangers to one
another. I sat next to a window, and Mr. Watkins, wife, and child were seated next to me.

When all were still the curtains were opened
by the spirit "Priscilla," who appeared and
blessed the circle and retired to the cabinet, when
"Bright Eyes" and Mr. Holland, two others of
Mrs. Williams' "spirit guides," also greeted the
assembled guests. Immediately after they had
withdrawn another radiant spirit opened the curtains and earnestly beckoned to Mr. Watkins, who
approached, and they held a conversation for several minutes. At its close this spirit drew the curtains wider apart, and taking Mr. Watkins' arm,
walked with him to the middle of the room, and
addressing the circle in a soft but clear voice, said,
"I am *his* control, and the guide of his mediumship," and *instantly* vanished from our sight
where she was standing!

The next scene thrilled and delighted us all;
for as the curtains opened there stood the majestic
form with which art has made the whole world so
familiar, and the entire circle exclaimed, as with
one voice, "*Dr. Franklin!*" The proverbial

dress in every particular detail, as well as the grand and benignant countenance and graceful gesture of head, gently bowed and extended arm, all bespoke the unmistakable presence of the immortal Philosopher, Statesman, and Philanthropist. After a few moments of dignified and pleasing recognition of his reception, to my great surprise he turned and beckoned me to approach, which I did with a strange feeling of reverence and awe, and looking beamingly with his large benevolent eyes as he moved up still closer to me, said in a clear voice :

" Tell the old lady of this place, that we appreciate all that she and her deceased husband have done, and all that she herself is now doing for the cause of Spiritualism. Tell her this." (The old lady referred to was Mrs. Alden then in her eighty-seventh year. She and her deceased husband had been devoted spiritualists for thirty years.)

I had hardly resumed my seat before the sage advanced a little, and courteously addressed the circle in these words :

" I am here to prove the truth of Spirit return.

When I was in mortal life I was a medium.   God bless you all."

It were vain to try to impart to the reader any adequate conception of the feelings of those who witnessed this scene, and heard Franklin's words.

During the entire *séance* the light from the chandelier was bright enough to read by, and neither then nor afterward was any doubt expressed of the genuineness of the manifestations by any one who was present that evening ; and among them were many who openly declared themselves not only sceptics when they came, but incorrigible disbelievers in Spiritualism—they had regarded it as the work of fanatics and impostors. But during the two weeks I spent there as a close observer, I did not meet one person, among the multitudes who attended these *séances*, that did not end in adopting the belief of direct intercourse between the living and their departed friends.   And I will further add that, with unusual facilities for observation in many countries, among enlightened circles of men and women, have I ever met with a larger proportion of individuals apparently better qualified to examine the claims of any new subject of investigation than I met at Lake Cassadagua.

I should be sorry to omit one or two other incidents which I witnessed during these *séances*, for one had a peculiar interest to all observers, and another to myself, for reasons which will be quite apparent to any reader who happens to remember the interest I felt in the workman who put up Mrs. Williams' cabinet and was allowed to inspect her " tools in trade." He was to act as detective-in-chief for the exposure of "the humbug " for the good of mankind. He could not be " sold "; he had built that cabinet ; he knew all about it, and he and the boys were coming. If Mrs. Williams could fetch up his dead rich old uncle, and tell what became of his money, why then there might be something *to* it—otherwise ! well, etc."

I had something else better to do than to watch the progress of his search after his dead uncle, and the detective and his millionnaire passed out of my mind until at one evening *séance* I happened to see him seated near the door—from which, it occurred to me, he thought he could readily escape if anything fearful should happen. He watched everything going on with a kind of feline sagacity and patience, till at last, at the opened curtain, he saw a little figure looking directly at him, and beckoning him to come to her. The skeptic foreman seemed to recognize the child ; he slowly rose and made his way through the circle till he reached the spot, and stooping to look closer, the angelic girl threw her white arms around his neck, and exclaimed.

" Oh ! dear, dear father, don't you know your loving child ? "

He raised her, and clasped her to his breast, where he held her for a few moments in full sight of the whole circle, when she suddenly vanished into thin air, and with an astonished, vacant look all around him, and a big bandanna handkerchief pressed to his face, he made his way as best he could back to his seat. There was (to me) so much of the serio-comic in the scene, that I pressed *my* handkerchief to my face to keep from laughing. Poor fellow ! If he had lost a rich uncle he had found an angel daughter.

The other incident I alluded to happened at

the second public *séance* of Mrs. Williams. The room was full. Not far from me sat a young man of engaging appearance, and near him an elderly lady dressed in mourning, and between them a lovely girl of some four or five years, whose rich flowing golden hair and beautiful face had excited everybody's admiration. Never having seen before so young a person at such an assembly, I feared that something might happen to disturb the circle, and I afterward learned that others felt the same apprehension. But nothing occurred to justify our fears, and finally we had probably forgotten the little one's existence, other marvellous scenes demanding our constant and absorbed attentions.

At last the curtains were folded aside, and a transcendentally beautiful spirit appeared, clothed in purest white drapery, which floated around her delicate form, and casting her glistening eyes in the direction of the young man, the elderly lady and the child, earnestly beckoned them toward her. The three moved, and the group stood before the spirit, when she cried in a tender but clear voice :

" Let me—Oh! let me see my child."

The young man (who proved to be its father) held the child up and set it on the table that stood in front of the cabinet near the spirit-mother, when she threw her arms around it, and in a sobbing voice said :

" Oh ! my own Ellen ! my dear child ! your mother—your *own* mother *is* here."

On a wave of the mother's hand the father then took his daughter back to their seat, while the elderly lady remained conversing with the spirit who proved to be her own daughter.

The whole scene moved the entire circle too deeply to be regarded as anything but a demonstrated reality; for it was too actual and too lifelike and tender to be either resisted or forgotten.

When the circle broke up, several ladies and gentlemen gathered around the calm, bright little girl, and one of them asked her :

" Who was that beautiful lady who spoke to you and embraced you ? "

She replied, with an almost angry look, as she pointed to her father and grandma :

" *They* told me mamma was dead."

" And is she not dead ? "

" Why ! didn't you see her take me in her arms, and kiss me, and call me her dear little Ellen, as she used to ! and so papa and grandma mustn't tell me again that mamma is dead. And she promised to be with me and watch over me as long as I lived, and I know she will do it."

The parties here spoken of reside at Jamestown, New York, and if they ever see this book they will at once recognize the accuracy of this statement.

7

XIV.

THE RETURN TO NEW YORK.

OUR *Villegiatura* came to an end, and we were glad to be once more settled in our comfortable home. But I had by no means given up the idea of prosecuting my investigations into the great subject of Spiritualism, which had not mastered *me*—I was determined to master *it*.

I did not expect to solve all its mysteries, nor perhaps *any* of them which involved this immense subject. But I was not appalled at the difficulties. I treated it as I had all other problems for investigation.

I was after facts. I cared for nothing else ; though I must confess I had been far better rewarded in my search for them, in this so-called ''mystic field'' than I had been in many other departments of study—particularly in what are classed among the ascertainable facts of physics, like astronomy, or the unsatisfactory problems of government, or sociology.

I was seeking for light on *the greatest of all problems—the life to come after our mortal life closes; if there be an after life, what kind of a life will that be ? How can we learn something of all this ? Who can know except those who have gone there ? And amongst the innumerable myriads of the departed, who so likely to come and tell us as they who knew and loved us here ?* And so through the almost endless range of questions which every soul of earth asks. How can we get these questions answered except by direct communion with the departed, whom we *know* to have left their mortal bodies to the earth, and who at our invocation return to prove that we too are immortal ?

XV.

AT HOME.

I COULD now carry out my purpose with freedom from interruption or disturbance, and I had abundant leisure for my work. Besides, I felt calmness of mind now to be able to bring to the occupation my best powers for learning the simple truth. I was not conscious of any other desire, nor of any prejudice to sway my judgment or bias my feelings. I felt that for me the period of illusions had passed. Not that I had outgrown all susceptibility to romance, much less to the ideal, in which we all love to indulge ; but the fascinations of a mundane life had paled before the rising splendors of the enduring life to come.

I at once glided gladly into the restful routine of home, with no cares except those which I voluntarily assumed for others, whose needs I could

supply or sorrows I might alleviate. And thus I
rested, content to await what further developments
might come.

In looking over cards, notes, and messages that
may have been sent in my absence from town, my
eyes fell upon one of special interest. It was from
a lady I had been very intimate with in Paris on
my last visit. I called at her hotel, and we had a
long talk about former times and all that had happened to us since. I had known her to be a confirmed Spiritualist, and a woman of exquisite culture—a class so numerous in France but so rare
in other countries. In our former intercourse she
had indicated in a curious way her spiritualistic
tendencies, but not clearly enough to be very
well understood by one who could not respond
very definitely to her shadowy belief. So our
conversation had floated away from such themes,
to be resumed if fortune should ever bring us together again.

I said, " I know *now* what you sometimes hint-
ed at in those delightful times, and I fancy we
shall understand each other far better if I tell you
that since we parted, I have carefully investigated

those matters, and I am as thoroughly convinced of the truth of Spiritualism as I am of anything else in the world." My friend rose and embraced me more warmly than when we had met a few minutes before, and as her fine face lit up with a brilliant glow she said, "Now, *ma chere*, we can talk understandingly. Tell me all."

I traced my progress from darkness and doubt, to light and certainty, and related some of the more impressive scenes I had witnessed in spiritual demonstrations. She was delighted but not much surprised, for her experience had long antedated my own in this sphere, and therefore she entered with warmer sympathy into my own.

In this case, as in so many others, my allotted space restricts my recitals within very narrow limits. She told me how rapidly Spiritualism had spread throughout France, and especially among the ranks of the higher classes, where *savants* treated it as much a settled science as any of the established propositions in the realm of demonstrated physics.

" The philosophy and solutions often engage

the keenest discussion, but the endless phenomena have ceased to be questioned."

" But," I inquired, " how closely do the French phenomena correspond with ours of which you have read so much ? "

" Why, Spiritualism must be substantially the same thing everywhere it is developed; but with many exceptions (as for instance with the American colony in Paris) the French Spiritualists seem to idealize the significance of the plain facts into something still more subtle and spiritualistic than Spiritualism itself. I hardly know if you can exactly take my meaning, for although I am told that I speak English pretty well, I feel more at home in my own tongue."

She dropped into French (which I will try to render into English for the general reader) and continued with increased earnestness and fervor :

" It is perhaps owing to the peculiar genius of my countrymen ; but while they are the most *spirituelle* of all peoples, they discard your term Spiritualists, and call themselves *Spirites*, and generally entertain the idea of the *reincarnation of the soul in a new body after death.*"

" Then are *you* a reincarnationist ? "

" Not by any means—so far as I understand the term."

" But what do the reincarnationists mean by that word ? "

" They do not doubt the immortality of the soul, for they believe in continued life in other material and human forms after the soul has passed away."

" But not that they change so that their *identity* is so lost to those who knew them that they could no longer recognize and greet them as old friends ? "

" Not that exactly, perhaps. But rather that their immortality in prolonged existence will be in renewed physical life here."

" For what purpose ? "

" They think that in this way untold millions of earth's mortals—especially those who pass to a spirit life in infancy—and others unnumbered, only slightly developed intellectually, will have a further opportunity for advancement in the spheres by such experience on earth."

" I confess I see no satisfactory reasons or necessity for such a belief. I know that some such

idea existed among the old Greeks and the me-
tempsychosists, or transmigration of the soul into
some other animal form. But I did not know
that such a notion had found a place outside of
ancient mythology, and its dreamy superstitions.
I have never found a hint of such a thing from
any of my spirit friends, nor do I see any reason
for it. I see no necessity for it. How can any
soul once emancipated from the hard bondage of
earthly conditions, ever desire to resume its former servitude? They may desire to enjoy the
freedom of coming back to bring aid and comfort
to their loved ones who are still struggling along,
as they did, through the sorrows and troubles of
earth, *as we know* they do return. But I hope
these hallucinations do not prevail extensively
among the French Spiritualists, least of all in your
own mind."

"Oh, no. I think that this life is the first stage
of immortal existence; that when we leave this
state we advance forever. This is my meaning of the word ' Spiritualism.' But," she continued, "I wanted to tell you of a strange thing
which happened before I left France. I had gone

to pass two weeks with a dear friend of mine, the
Countess De N——, at her beautiful chateau in
Normandy, and as we drifted one evening into
the marvellous, she related to me the following incident, which would be hardly worth telling
except to show how often our spirit friends try to
commune with us and have to go away disappointed.

" Ten years had passed by since the occurrence
took place, and although she knew all the time
that I was a Spiritualist, she felt a reluctance to
speak of it, for fear she might be considered weak-
minded or superstitious ; and she might well feel
sensitive on this point, for she was one of the leaders of the most brilliant circles of Paris.

" ' But,' she said, ' I can tell you all about this
strange incident, and while you will never repeat
it perhaps, you may solve the mystery, since you
are supposed to understand such things.

" ' *Eh bien !* About ten years ago the viscount,
my husband, who always slept in my room, rose
as usual at 5 o'clock in the morning at the sound
of the alarm, for he had the habit of rising at that
hour summer and winter, and retiring to the li-

brary to begin his scientific studies. It now being mid-winter, it would have been entirely dark had I not kept a lamp burning in my adjoining dressing-room, which cast a subdued light into my sleeping-chamber, but sufficient to reveal all objects distinctly.

" ' Shortly after the count retired each morning, my *femme de chambre* always brought me a cup of coffee, and set it on the little stand at the side of my bed, and seeing I was awake she withdrew.

" ' I lay awake for some time longer than usual, and reaching out my hand for the coffee my eyes were arrested by the sight of a man sitting in a chair at the foot of the bed ; and then I recognized my granduncle, the Baron L——, as plain as I ever saw him in life, and he had been dead and buried in the family vault for thirty years ! It was so real that for a moment I forgot the lapse of time and everything else, and in my irrepressible joy at the thought of seeing the old man again whom I had so dearly loved from my girlhood, I rose in bed and exclaimed, " Oh ! how are you, my dear old uncle ! "

" ' " Well! well, my dear child ! I have come back to see you."

" ' In an instant I recalled the past and asked : "Having been dead thirty long years, how can it be you ? and yet I know it is."

" ' I was overwhelmed with terror. The great drops of cold sweat stood on my head, and I trembled in every limb. He was approaching closer to me. I pulled the counterpane over my head, and yet I felt him coming closer and closer to my head, when I must have uttered an agonizing scream, for it brought my maid to my bed, who bathed my forehead and wept in terror. " What, oh ! what, dear countess, has happened ? "

" ' I gazed at the foot of the bed ; the chair was vacant: my uncle was gone and I had frightened him away ! Then a grief came over me of which I could not give you the faintest conception. I knew then, and I have known ever since, that it was no nightmare, no nervous fancy. I know it was my dear old uncle, and oh ! how many, many times have I longed to see him. But he has never come back.' "

" Well," I asked, "can you tell me the rest ?

There ought to be some interesting *dénouement* to this story.

"'I may give it to you hereafter, for I am persuaded that it will come.' But I left the countess the next morning, and sailed two days afterward for New York. Of course I could say something *apropos* on the subject. But I mention it only to show how anxious our departed friends are to resume converse with us, and how difficult they often find it to be understood when they do their best. But both they and we are making progress, and soon, I think, the two worlds will be drawn much closer together."

XVI.

BEFORE I come to the relation of some things which subsequently happened in my own experience after returning to New York, I wish to speak of something which may possess a deeper interest to a larger class of readers in America and Europe, since they concern the spirit life of certain persons whose fame has filled the world. I will introduce a few incidents which, if the names were given, would command as much respect as those of Professors Wallace, or Crooke, or De Morgan, who fearlessly, years ago, pronounced their full adhesion to the system of Spiritualism as now adopted throughout the learned world.

The gentleman of whom I speak, if I should give his name, would at once be recognized as one of the foremost of living American historians, and one of the most admired and respected of scientific writers on the great social questions which are now commanding the earnest attention of the thinkers of our times. I invoke for his statements the same confidence that I know my personal friends will give to my own. I preserve his account in his own words.

"It was well known that Napoleon III. had for many years given time and attention enough to an exhaustive investigation of the phenomena and philosophy of Spiritualism, and that he was aided in this work by some of the most eminent *savants* of France and other countries, particularly the United States, where the study had been so early extensively cultivated. It was the habit of that extraordinary man to gather facts on any subject he was investigating, from every reliable quarter before he reached a conclusion. Having been myself engaged in a historical literary work which concerned the Bonaparte family, our correspondence had led to an unusually familiar acquaintance, and at his desire I arranged the best series of tests which I could devise, to solve or dismiss the doubts of any scholar or scientist who was disposed to examine one phase of the alleged proofs of intercourse between the *minds* of the living and the departed, without reference to any of the common physical phenomena.

" Some months before the trial was to take place, I had selected from an autographic collection six letters which most intimately concerned myself as well as the personal private history of the six writers, and enclosing them in separate colored envelopes exactly alike, without any mark, sign, or endorsement by which they could be distinguished from each other, even by myself, I threw them together, and after an hour's walk from my office I returned and enclosed them all in one envelope securely sealed by my own seal ring which had no duplicate, when I laid them aside in a secret drawer of my safe where no one but myself could get access without my consent.

" Several months went by, and I selected from among my intimate acquaintance, separately, six of the most thoroughly learned and scientific men in New York, all of whom I knew to have no belief in Spiritualism, and who could never have been persuaded, except by a personal friend, to act as experts in the business of determining the question *whether the dead could satisfactorily prove that they could and would hold direct intercourse with the living.* They understood that they were to sit as a jury of scientific experts, and bring in an impartial verdict according to the evidence. After much persuasion, each consenting to serve after being duly summoned, and neither knowing the names of the other five, I set about to fix on a medium for an appointment when we were to have an uninterrupted *séance.*

"To accomplish this *perfectly,* I had to consult only one other person, and she the 'one altogether lovely' to me as a ministering spirit—*Theodosia Burr Alston,* whose mysterious death at sea had excited the sympathy of the world, partly because she was the daughter of Colonel Aaron Burr, the Vice-President of the United States, and under whose fatal shot Alexander Hamilton had needlessly fallen in a duel which was forced by the two angry political parties on the antagonists. This had given accidental notoriety to her name; but being one of the most beautiful, accomplished, and

8

lovely women in the world of her time, she had won the admiration and devoted love of all who knew her.

" While I was sitting with the medium I wrote her a sealed note, and as the medium's hand touched it he began the answer. (I will explain that Theodosia was a blood cousin of mine, and although she had died some years before I was born, yet she must have known—as spirits know —my motives, since my object was to bring to-gether some of our blood.) The answer said :

" ' *Dear Cousin :* I will manage the matter. Next Sun-day I will bring the entire band you desire, and we will all meet you and your circle in this room, at eleven o'clock in the morning.   Your affectionate
            " ' THEODOSIA BURR ALSTON.'

" This was enough for me. I made the appoint-ment with the medium and hurried away to inform each of my experts of the time and place by letter, all of whom responded the next day. I awaited the result with confidence. No intimation of my full purpose had escaped my lips. No mortal knew it. My secret was known to only one being, and that was the beautiful spirit Theodosia. Even the medium knew only of the engagement for the following Sunday. To avoid all mistakes, I saw all my six friends in the latter part of the week and renewed the appointment, and on Saturday I opened my safe and took the package from the inner drawer and carried it home.

" At the appointed hour the next morning we all met, and we were *all* together for the first time. No one knew anything beyond what I had been obliged to say to each as a justification for my strange request.

" I then explained the facts I have already narrated, and drew forth the package from my pocket, and only one person in the room could have surmised from mortal source the contents of that package.

" The six envelopes were spread out on the medium's table, and he was told that one contained a document in the handwriting of a dead person, and I wished to see if the spirits of these people would, through his own hand, prove by their responses that they knew the contents of the envelopes, and identify themselves as being the authors of the letters.

"It was agreed by the company that if all the conditions had been faithfully represented, they did not see how any collusion or deception could have taken place. They did not know the medium, but they knew me too well to suppose me capable of so stupendous a fraud in the sacred name of science ; and perhaps, after all, who knew ? At any rate they wouldn't judge in advance.

"To the proof—*allons !* The six sat around in a crescent, and but an occasional word was uttered during two hours. The medium began by running his hand over the envelopes, and at last it was arrested and he commenced to write rapidly. As a sheet slid from the table, one of the party pinned it to the first envelope and marked it No. 1. Then the next pinned its answer to No. 2, and so on till the entire six had been disposed of, and each lay before the half circle. Every man had one before him on the carpet. Then by agreement No. 1 was raised and torn from the envelope and read aloud by the reader, and the answer read by his neighbor. This comparison was most critically made by all present, and there was but one judgment expressed—only one solution to the problem proposed in the beginning—viz., that nothing seemed so rational as to accept the conclusion that, as the replies to the letters corresponded with the originals so closely and logically, as did the handwriting in every case, they could not fairly refuse to acknowledge the truth of the demonstration.

"It is only proper to remark that it led in each case to further investigations with the same and other mediums, until all these gentlemen declared themselves unalterably convinced of the fact of direct intercourse between the living and the dead."

XVII.

HOW I WAS GUIDED TO THE "FORREST HOME" BY LUCILLE WESTERN TO FIND HER MOTHER.

HAVING been invited by Mrs. Williams to a dark circle with a few personal friends, among several impressive displays of remarkable spirit power, a most unexpected one came to myself. The room was perfectly dark during the entire *séance*, but each sitter was favored in her turn by visitors who seemed to make themselves fully known by conversation, which has always had a special charm for me, for it is so clear a proof of the intercourse of *mind with mind* through one sense alone—that of *hearing*.

Close to my ear came these words: " The gates are no longer ajar, my dear Kate ; they are wide open."

" Who is it that is speaking?" I asked. The answer came instantly :

" *Lucille Western.* Don't you remember me?"

" Of course I do ;" and well I might, for we had been children together in Boston.

Then after a pause she said :

" Oh! how I wish dear mother could know of all this."

I asked, " Where is she, Lucille?"

" In the ' Forrest Home,' near Philadelphia."

I then promised that I would go to see her as soon as I could, and with her warmest thanks Lucille withdrew. Certain engagements prevented me for some time from fulfilling my pledge, and I thought I would write a letter to Mrs. Western. But what could I write? I had not heard or thought of her for years, and had I known the old lady was living, I could not have guessed in what part of the universe she was. But Lucille had told me, and I knew she always spoke the truth ; and besides, she *must* know all about it.

But I delayed writing until shortly afterward, when I attended a light circle at Mrs. Williams' one evening, where an unusually large number of highly cultured persons were present, and all the conditions to insure success seemed to be combined.

In the midst of the evening's *séance* suddenly a brilliantly attired and beaming form came forth from the cabinet, which was as instantly recognized as she had ever been in coming out from the side scenes of the stage, and many in the circle who had known her involuntarily exclaimed :

" *That is Lucille Western ;* " and they were not mistaken—they could not be mistaken.   Least of all could I, for she asked for me and we met, when she whispered in my ear, clearly :

" In writing to mother, tell her that it was I who caused her to have that strange dream she had the other night.   These words will prove your *open sesame.*"

That very night my letter was posted.   I only signed it " A Friend," but said I should shortly visit her.   But before starting I had another interview with Lucille, who told me that her mother had received my letter and was anxious to know who could have written it.   I assured Lucille that I should shortly make the visit.   So I started for Philadelphia, with a lady companion, under spirit

guidance, and at our hotel inquired for the " Forrest
Home," but they could give me no information.
But as railway agents are so apt to know about
locations, I inquired at the Broad Street Station,
where the ticket agent very obligingly gave me
all the directions. We took the 1 P.M. train, and
after a ride of thirteen miles found ourselves at the
nearest station to the Home, which was reached
by an omnibus in a mile and a half. Passing the
gateway we found ourselves in a park of old oaks,
in which stood an imposing stone mansion, which
with its surroundings reminded me of an English
baronial seat. At the door we inquired for Mrs.
Western with as much confidence as though I had
followed a mortal instead of a spirit guide.

" Yes, ladies ; if you will step into the parlor I
will call her."

I soon heard a familiar voice—although so many
years had gone by.

An elderly woman entered, attired in the subdued but very tasteful dress of an accustomed
lady, and I introduced myself as coming at the
request of her daughter *Lucille*.

" Yes !" she said ; " but you know *Lucille* is

no longer among the living. Oh! I begin to see. You must be my unknown correspondent who spoke of a dream. Yes, I did have a very wonderful dream, and I was a good deal perplexed about it. I must tell you of it."

She did; and we soon began to understand each other better. I then said, " Don't you recollect Kate? I am she."

" You really are she?"

" I am," I replied, " and your daughter *Lucille* is still living, and I have conversed with her probably twenty times within two months. The last time she told me to say that she caused you to have that strange dream, and to tell you that it would be a very great comfort to her if you could only know that she was with you, and loved you better if possible than ever, and that if she could have an opportunity she would *prove* it all to you. Now, my dear Mrs. Western, as I have been guided here only by the spirit of our dear Lucille, and have brought all these proofs to you, pray tell me what you think of it?"

" Why, what *can* I think, but that it is so—— it must be true?"

I shall not attempt to describe the joyous emotion that lit up her beautiful face. After many questions she said :

" Now let me summon our lady guests and tell them what a strange and delightful occurrence has happened, for it is certainly the most unexpected and wonderful event of my life."

" The ladies "—and they were fully worthy of being so called—were introduced to us one after another, and when they were seated Mrs. Western told the entire story, neglecting not a single incident, dream and all, before an audience of old-time actresses who had played so many parts so many years before, and so well, that they had fairly won their places of honor in this superb and palatial " Forrest Home," founded by that prince of actors by the labors and savings of a long and brilliant life dedicated to the noble histrionic art which has from the time of Sophocles, done so much to delight, amuse, and elevate mankind.

" It was such a scene as could have hardly ever before been enacted on the earth." These were the words of the lady friend I had brought with me, and who, having no knowledge of my special

purpose, and no real idea of Spiritualism, and consequently no enlightened belief in it. " How wonderful all this is," she exclaimed ; and so said they
all.

They were amazed ! " It was a strange per-
formance, at least," said one. " Very wonderful,"
exclaimed another. " And yet we were not dream-
ing, were we ? " asked a third. " What can it
mean ? We have all impersonated fairies, ghosts,
hobgoblins, and sprites—but have we ever *seen*
any of these actual beings ? "

The conclusion was, however, reached. " What
could be so splendid as to have some such thing
enacted in our little theatre ? Oh ! if we only
could. Mrs. K——, is it possible ? Could you
possibly bring about so magnificent a miracle ? "

I could hardly make any such promise. But
we agreed we would look for something strange
but real in the near future ; and so we *underlined
the new play as in preparation.* We felt that we
must go, and we bade this band of retired actresses
who had delighted so many hearts, in so many
lands, in so many scenes and for such long years,
farewell, and the curtain fell. It may rise again.

XVIII.

GENERAL GARIBALDI RETURNS FROM THE SPIRIT LAND.

I HAD now and then thought, how great a satisfaction it would be to see General Garibaldi, and hold a conversation with him, as I and my husband had during a special visit which we made, at his earnest invitation, to his home at Caprera.

Something of what my husband had done to aid the cause of Italy in her great struggle for independence and union, especially in enabling Generals Avezzana and Garibaldi, both of them being then exiles in New York, to return to help their country, is all so well known to the world, that I hope I shall not be thought guilty of pride or ostentation in these allusions, as they seem to be necessary to show why I had grown so anxious once more to see the great apostle of liberty since his translation to the Spirit Land.

In attending another *séance* of our usual kind, shortly after my last interview with Professor Agassiz, I was not surprised to hear the familiar voice of spirit Holland—one of Mrs. Williams' spirit guides—announce that " my old friend General Garibaldi was present, and would appear to me that evening."

I was agitated by the most inspiring hopes and tender recollections as I recalled the circumstances of our memorable visit to Caprera—shall I be forgiven if I recall them ? .

Our European tour was about to close with a pilgrimage to the home of the greatest of the modern Italians. On our way we stopped at Florence to seek out my husband's old friend General Avezzana, who was reposing from his battles in an honored seat in the Parliament of the nation which he had done so much to save.

The General and his daughter Katie greeted us with all the ardor of Italian friendship, and immediate preparations were made for a trip to Caprera.

With a party of invited guests we set sail from Leghorn in the steamship Elba, chartered for the purpose, and skirting the shores of Elba and Corsica, we reached Caprera after a delightful *viaggetta* of eighteen hours.

On approaching the shore we first saw the Garibaldi house, and next a group of persons standing on a rock not far from the landing. On a nearer view we recognized the General himself as the central figure, resting on his crutches, surrounded by his staff officers.

The General had on the costume made so familiar by his pictures—the red shirt, and black neckerchief tied in a sailor's knot and hanging down his back, wide gray pants, and a peculiar overgarment of cloth, something like a Roman toga. He wore a small round cap embroidered with gold, and taking him just as he appeared then, one would say he was a man about fifty-five, with light brown hair and small brown eyes, and something more of the lion in his face than the pictures give him. His manners were courteous and full of dignity.

Avezzana approached the General, and after

embracing each other like two long-parted broth-
ers, Avezzana presented all the parties by name,
and Garibaldi putting his arm through mine on
one side, and Avezzana's on the other, took the
lead to the house, as if desirous of welcoming the
party himself.

The house was as unpretentious as its master—
bespeaking fellowship and hospitality without ostentation.   The edifice was built of stone and
rubble, like most Italian country houses of the
present day, of two stories, with a hall in the
middle and rooms on either side.

After the guests were seated at the table, the
host remarked that " what they saw was the pro-
duct of his little island—wines, flowers, fruits,
vegetables, and meats."

One of the savory dishes of the abundant re-
past was part of a wild goat which the General had
shot the day before, not very far from his house.

It was a primitive but most impressive scene,
the like of which no one present was likely ever
to see again.

And this was Garibaldi of Caprera.   Years had
rolled by, and now the same man who had, at

what we miscall death—which only opened to him
the gates to immortality—come back to our mundane sphere, and talked as of old, of the life he
led then, and the life he was leading now among
his celestial peers.

These recollections were suddenly dispelled at
this *séance* by hearing my name called, when before the curtain stood General Garibaldi as I had
seen him twelve years before at his island home !

At a sign of recognition I approached him, and
he greeted me as warmly as in mortal life, and
called me by the name he used to call me, " Gentle Katie." Then for some minutes he spoke with
his old enthusiasm about Italy and " the sacred
cause of liberty " for which he had lived and died.

I asked him if he remembered when we parted.

" Oh ! yes ; how well ! " and putting his large
arm around my waist, he said, in a voice loud
enough for the entire circle to hear, and in full
sight of all :

" Yes, at Caprera, and with my arm around
your waist as I have it now ; " and then, like so
many dear ones, he vanished from my sight.

9

XIX.

SOON after returning from my delightful visit to the " Forrest Home," I was favored with a call from one of my old friends whom I had not seen for some time, and he happened to allude to the investigation of Spiritualism at Harvard College, before Professor Felton, about twenty-six years ago. This at once excited my interest, for knowing that the Professor was a brother-in-law of Professor Louis Agassiz of the same university, I listened very attentively to an account of that examination in the presence of two such eminent *savants*, with whom my friend had been so intimately acquainted. He said :

" A body of intellectual and scientific men of Cambridge and Boston, who had carefully examined into the alleged phenomena of Spirit-

ualism, desired to bring the subject to the attention of the *savants* of Harvard University, and
they proposed to present the proofs to the two
eminent professors, Agassiz and Felton. The
latter gentleman, after very persistent pressure,
consented, but with great reluctance, to preside,
and did; but Agassiz only consented to be present as an *observer*. The meeting was held, and
the 'exhibition' went on, and was so success-
ful that Professor Felton confessed that he 'saw
no evidence of trick or collusion, and while he
certainly was not disposed to deny what he saw,
and could not admit that it was in any sense the
work of spirits, he was totally unable to account
for it by any laws or processes with which he was
acquainted.'

"An appeal was then made to Professor Agassiz,
who had from his position been a close observer,
and he replied that 'he thought he could explain
it all,' and he promised to do so at some future
time. But as far as my information extends, he
never announced that he had done so; and although he was repeatedly pressed to attend circles and converse with mediums by many of his

fellow-scientists, and other men and women for whose opinions and statements on *other* subjects he showed the greatest deference, yet he always avoided any discussion of Spiritualism—with him it was ' a matter as utterly beyond the pale of scientific discussion, as the construction of a machine to produce perpetual motion.' "

All this, so positively asserted by my eminently learned friend, and from his own personal knowledge, almost confounded me, for it seemed to me so utterly unlike the scientific spirit or mode of philosophical investigation for which Professor Agassiz was so pre-eminently distinguished, that I resolved, if possible, to find out his present views on the subject; for he had been some five or six years in the spirit world, where he would have had the matter *forced* on his attention, and I could neither doubt his candor to confess his mistake, nor his desire to illuminate his fellow-men.

I could not repress the desire to see and converse with my illustrious guest and the friend of my husband, for I knew them both to be in the spirit state, and it would be passing strange if they had not met each other before now. If I could reach my point in no other way, I believed my husband would hunt up the Professor, and sooner or later bring about a meeting.

Two evenings after the conversation just related, I attended a private *séance* with Mrs. Williams, and after many of my familiar friends had come and retired, the curtains opened and there, under full gaslight, stood Professor Agassiz, his perfect self, as actual as life, and as unmistakable as I had looked at him times without number in our house, and in walking around our grounds. Beckoning me to him as he came forth from the cabinet, with his grand form and genial smile, I gladly went to him and said :

" Dear Professor, how glad I am you have come ! "

" I heard what you said to your friend about your desire to see me, and so I am here. But it is still a mystery to me. I do not fully understand it yet."

" And still you are here, we both know, which proves the truth of spirit return."

" *Yes, it is so ;* and I want my old friends in Cambridge also to know it."

" But how, Professor ? "

" Why, through none other than yourself, madam ; " and pressing his hand on my left shoulder, said, " No one better." And then in my presence, as I was standing close to him, and with that pressure of his hand yet on my shoulder, he vanished without moving away.

My joy was indescribable !

XX.

THE USES OF SPIRITUALISM.

MANY persons, while obliged to concede the probable truth of spirit return, ask :

" Well, if it be all so, what good is it to those who believe already in immortality? Is there any practical benefit in it to the believer? Does it improve their conduct, and make them lead better lives ? "

I will relate a single instance, out of a large number I have known, which shows how beneficent an influence this belief exerts on human character here in our every-day life.

As this subject came up in a conversation, not long ago, with a well-known gentleman of high standing in the great world of business in New York, he used the following language :

" For many years I had been immersed in the

hot pursuit of trade and speculation, and had accumulated a fortune large enough to satisfy the reasonable ambition of any man ; for being left with only one child, I had enough for our support, and to enrich her if she should marry and have a home of her own. My daughter, who was yet hardly thirteen, was successfully pursuing her education, and with her fine constitution, my affection and pride were all centred on my lovely Ellen.

" Beyond a long life of independence and gratification for myself, and securing a happy settlement for Ellen, I neither desired nor expected anything better in this life, and as for another life, I *knew* nothing of it and I scarcely gave it a thought. When the subject came up I gave it no serious consideration, thinking I could not alter matters, and would run my chances with the rest.

" So I determined to go on with my accustomed pursuits. I found that the faster my wealth increased the more pleasure I felt in its accumulation, and the more consideration it gave me among the rapidly increasing class of very rich men with whom my means and business reputation brought me into close relations.

" My idea of wealth expanded with its increase, as did my ambition for a still more splendid settlement for my daughter. In the meantime I watched with greater pride her development into budding womanhood. Not a cloud hung over the future, and I thought myself one of the happiest and most fortunate of men.

" Suddenly, as if it were a bolt of lightning from a clear sky, the only calamity that could strike me fell : my daughter sickened and died. I can never give another the faintest conception of my misery. The light of life went out, and for a while I felt like one groping in the dark. I could find consolation nowhere. My brain seemed no longer to obey my will—I *had* no will—no purpose, no desire. Often since, I have thought I was going mad : not raving as people are when they have to be confined, but passing into a doleful state of nothingness.

" The housekeeper sent for one of my intimate friends, who roused me from my lethargy and partially brought me to myself. He prevailed on me to accompany him down town. There I began to feel myself again. Other friends dropped in. My confidential clerk brought out some wine and liquors from the private closet, and we fell back into old-time conversation, and agreed to meet the next day.

" Perhaps all this may have saved me from idiocy or insanity. Reaching home, other old friends happened in, and after long talks they left me. Relaxing into slumber I found oblivion in a dreamless sleep.

" Late the next morning I was waked for breakfast, and I ate the first substantial food I had taken since I had laid away my child by the side of her dead mother.

" I had no other thing to interest me, and I welcomed the old occupations of business in which I could partially forget my sorrow, while with boon companions over the wine-cup, some of the old fascination of my former life came back again, and I began to breast myself up against adversity, and sought more than ever the society of my associates who alone helped me to forget my irreparable loss.

" But this life could not last ; my business demanded my attention. I was called to Philadelphia. I had determined to begin to restrict my affairs, and resolved, after making everything snug, to leave the business world, seeking what peace I could find elsewhere.

"On the train I found myself seated next to an old merchant friend, who happened, in speaking of what had recently occurred in his home circle, to say that he had met with a severe domestic affliction in the death of his only son—a bright youth of only fourteen, in whose promising future he had treasured up so many hopes.

"'But,' said he with a very genial smile, 'I am not entirely prostrated by the blow.'

"I could not help saying, 'You seem to bear up very philosophically under so great a loss as the death of your son.' Turning round and looking me full in the face, he said :

"'Why? Why? my dear friend! my boy is not *dead*—I both see and converse with him.'

"For a moment it occurred to me that my friend must be insane. But before we reached Philadelphia he convinced me that if ever there was a sane man, he was the man. I had known him long, and I had supreme faith in his business judgment and perfect veracity.

" It ended in his extorting from me a promise that I would, that very evening, attend a materializing *séance*, which I did.

" There, as an entire stranger, I sat witnessing many marvellous things, till finally I saw the very image of my little girl come to me, and throwing her arms around my neck exclaimed :

" ' Dearest papa ! I am with you, and I see everything you do, and hear everything you say. I am not dead—there is no death. Do you know me ? Am I your dear, dear Ellen ? '

" I did know it ; and while I was holding her to my breast she vanished away.

" As I left that room, I felt as though I had just waked from a dream. Did my dear spirit child *hear* all I said ? and does she know and see all I do ? and can she love me still ? Oh, how I longed for her love ! How I needed it !

" No sleep for me that night—but what comfort came to my poor lacerated heart !

" The next day I returned to my home in New York. It was a new home to me, and I began a new life. No more wine—no more fascination for the old pursuits—no more dream or ambition for vast wealth—no more darkness in the future after death—there was no more death—only a transition.

"I found all my daughter had said to me confirmed through other circles in New York, and I know it now as well, and I realize it more deeply than any other experiences in my whole life !

"I began at once to end all ventures, risks, or speculations. I was not as rich as many of my old associates ; but I had quite enough to busy me in seeing how to make the best use of it I could for the good of others who had, somehow, been overlooked in the distribution of the gifts of fortune.

"So I am really busy and happy, you may well believe. Now I know we shall live hereafter, and at last I have found the object of our life here."

XXI.

HOW MY EXPERIENCES IN SPIRITUALISM EXPANDED.

I HAD recently been visiting some friends near New York, and had often heard them speak of a daughter they had lost years before. But I knew nothing further than that it was on an ocean steamer.

Soon after, in the course of an evening *séance*, spirit Holland, in addressing me from the cabinet, said that a person by the name of Winn wished to speak to me. In a few moments a young girl parted the curtains and walked out on the floor, and spreading out her arms and moving them as though in the act of swimming to sustain herself on the water, she appeared to fall on her face. But recovering she walked back to the cabinet, motioning for me to follow her, which I did. In a weak but distinct voice she said:

" It is my first attempt to materialize myself since I reached the spirit world. I wish you to tell my brother Andrew that I can return, and I wish to communicate with my friends."

Although I felt sure it must be the lost daughter to whom the friends I had recently visited had alluded, I could not give her name, for everything would be too indefinite to justify me in saying anything about it. So I resolved to wait till something else should come. I saw her again in a light *séance*.

I afterward had a dark *séance* at my own house, and almost the first spirit to come gave me her name. It was *Ella Winn*. She asked me to promise to let her brother know it all, which I did of course, as I would redeem any pledge to a friend in the flesh.

I had now seen her twice, and I was quite prepared to describe her person accurately enough to identify her, and I called one afternoon at his office. He listened for some time while I was relating what she had told me, and giving her name, he seemed much overcome, and rising from his chair said, "All this is very strange."

"Would you like to see her?" I asked.

"Well, yes. But not now. I wish to think of it," and I withdrew.

At my next interview with Ella she said:

"I was present when you saw my brother. Your words made some impression on him, and it will all come out right. I thank you, dear sister;" and kissing me on my forehead continued: "I am one of your band now, and shall be with you very, very often hereafter."

I then inquired:

"Ella, do you see my *material* body when I come close to you, as I do now, or my *spiritual* body? For I am anxious to know."

"I see both, for I love you and can come into your *aura*."

"Then am I to suppose that all our loved ones can do the same?"

"Yes—but it is not given to *all* spirits; some can only see the spirit body."

She dissolved from sight. But it was delightful to know that I had her assurance that she had joined the spirit band of my friends and guides, who will be with me till earth-journey is ended and we all meet in the Better Land.

Surely " they *are* all guardian spirits sent forth to minister to the heirs of Eternal Life."

10

XXII.

WHO WAS PRISCILLA?

THIS spirit purports to be one of Mrs. Williams'
band, and frequently comes to open her light
public circles, and prepare the way for the appearance of the vast number of spirits who invariably follow. Her identity was for a long time
unknown, and was at last ascertained in the following manner.

Under the heading " A Remarkable Identification of an Ancient Spirit," the illuminated editor
of *Mind and Matter*, a very able spiritual jour-
nal—November 17, 1883—says :

Ever since Mrs. Mary E. Williams, of New York City,
has been developed as a medium for the production of full-
formed materializations of spirits, one spirit in particular
has, at every *séance*, or nearly so, been the first to appear.
This spirit always comes robed in a pure white flowing dress,

and appears as a most attractive young woman. She has given her name as Priscilla, but further she made no attempt to identify herself. She has always, in a few words, greeted the circle, and, if we mistake not, stated her object in being the first spirit to appear at each circle to be that it was to prepare the way for the materialization of other spirits. Why this gentle spirit so long withheld the facts which would have identified her we do not know, but infer that she was not equal to giving the long explanation that would have been required for that purpose. Be that as it may, her identity has now been established in a most remarkable manner, the facts concerning which we will now briefly relate. The readers of *Mind and Matter* need not be told of the long-continued series of communications from ancient spirits given through the remarkable, if not unparalleled, mediumship of Alfred James, which have, during the past three years and a half, been given from week to week in the columns of this paper.

At a sitting with Mr. James, on June 13th last, we received a communication purporting to come from the spirit of Montanus, the Phrygian ecstatic and founder of the remarkable ancient religious sect called Montanists. This communication we published in *Mind and Matter* of August 18th. At that time Mrs. Williams was absent in Canada, where she remained for some weeks. She had not seen the copy of *Mind and Matter* containing the communication from Montanus. On her return to her home, at 462 West Thirty-fourth Street, New York, her spirit guides told her to get the paper of August 18th and read the first communication given through Mr. James as published in that num-

ber.   Mrs. Williams had read none of the James communications printed up to that time, on account of their treating
of matters that did not interest her.   She therefore heard
the request with indifference and failed to comply with it.
Nearly two months elapsed, when again her guides made
the urgent request that she would look that number of the
paper up and read the communication from Montanus.
This she was reluctant to do, as a large number of papers
and publications had accumulated in the meantime.   This
time, however, reluctant as she was about the matter, the
request was so urgent and persistent that she was forced
to comply, and set about hunting up the paper, which after
considerable trouble she found, she receiving an electric
shock as she took the paper containing the communication
in her hand.   The name of Priscilla had been mentioned
as interested in having Mrs. W. to read the communication.
What was her surprise to read the following portion of the
communication :

" When I was on earth (A.D. 170) everything was un-
dergoing transition.   Old and effete idolatrous religions
were beginning to die out before that great question pro-
pounded by the patriarch of Chaldea, Jovinus (called in
your Old Testament Job), whose works I read, and which
bore the date of 2200 years before my time : ' If a man die
shall he live again ? '   I found it repeated in a little book
called ' The Analysis of Pythagorianism,' which was extant
at that time.   This set me to thinking, and I then resolved
to follow the direction of Pythagoras, in order to establish
communication with what were termed the manes of our
ancestors.   This, by the aid of two female mediums or ec-

statics, I accomplished. Their names were Priscilla and Maximilla ; and from what we received through those ec-statics, myself and followers became converts to the teach-ings of the great intelligences that controlled them. With the fervor of our race we started out together to prove what we asserted was true, by word and act. Even the most learned and influential priests could not make a stand against our facts. From A.D. 175 to 250 we increased so rapidly as a sect, in spite of the opposition of the priest-hood of other systems then known, that our meetings were suppressed by the ruling powers of different countries. We actually proved, at the time of making our statements, that the true light had lightened every one that cometh into the world, because it was equally available to man, woman, and child. The Montanists were the predecessors, or founders, of Eclecticism of Potamon, Ammonius Saccas, and their fol-lowers, which was a blending of Platonism and Pythago-rianism. One of the so-called Christian fathers, Origen, became a follower of mine. We had those phases of spir-itual phenomena called trance, healing, physical appear-ances, and other manifestations of spirit power. Maximilla was a healing medium ; *Priscilla a medium for materializa-tion and other physical phenomena ;* and I was the trance medium, and taught in a state of ecstacy. There was one phenomenon that was very impressive. We mediums be-came transfigured and illuminated, so that the people could with difficulty look upon us. I taught from the revised Buddhistic canons of the reign of Ardelos Babeker, which Apollonius brought from India. It was translated into the Phrygian dialect by a priest of Cybele."

A few days after this singular but conclusive identification of spirit, Priscilla, who is so important a spirit-helper at Mrs. Williams' *séances* as the remarkable Phrygian ecstatic, we attended a *séance* given by Mrs. Williams, at which the spirit Priscilla appeared as usual. After saluting the circle she called us to the cabinet, where we had the fullest opportunity of seeing the spirit fully, and have no doubt whatever that she is the same Priscilla that, with Montanus and Maximilla, more than seventeen hundred years ago, sought to resume the spiritualistic work of the Samian sage, Pythagoras, and who created such a commotion throughout the countries of Asia that were peopled by Greeks, and which spread over all the Greek and African provinces of the Roman Empire. We regard the identification of this ancient medium as positively certain. It is not the least significant feature of her present work that it is identically the same as it was when she lived on earth, that is giving proof to mortals that the spirits of the so-called dead do live, do return, and do actually manifest themselves to the physical senses of those of earth's inhabitants who have perception enough to receive the evidence that is made tangible to them.

It is a well-established fact now throughout the spiritualistic world, that many of the most illuminated philosophers and teachers of past ages are returning from the spirit spheres, and establishing their identity by the most irrefragable proofs. All this goes to show that the relations of the departed of former times with the living of this age are becoming more and more intimate. Nor is it too much to expect revelations from the chief actors of past generations, who will cast clear light upon the nations which flourished in the far-off antiquity, that has hitherto lain concealed in the mists of what we call the pre-historic periods.

XXIII.

LIFE AND OCCUPATIONS IN THE SPIRIT WORLD.

A VAST amount of information on this subject exists, and it is found scattered through the literature of all nations, embracing their records in print, manuscripts, traditions, and monuments which are being interpreted more and more clearly, as science and knowledge advance among mankind. But as these sources of information are open to investigation on all sides, I shall confine myself, as I proposed in the beginning, chiefly to what I have learned by my own experience and observation.

All through human history we find that mankind have felt an irrepressible yearning for knowledge of the life to come, especially of the conditions and pursuits of their departed friends. Since new light has in our new age begun to stream over this and many other occult subjects, our knowledge has been rapidly increasing, until the material and the spiritual worlds have been brought so close together that we can, and do, get as satisfactory knowledge of the life of humanity in a spirit state, as we do of our surroundings here.

Indeed, we venture to say even more ; for where the processes of chemistry in photography, and the manipulation of electro-magnetism in the telegraph and telephone, are comprehended by one operator, the relations of the minds of the living with the minds of the departed, are known and comprehended by thousands.

There *seems* to be a more subtle connection between the intercourse of mortals and spirits, but it is only in the *seeming;* for if ten or fifteen years ago it had been said that words uttered in New York would be instantly heard and answered at Chicago, it would have been pronounced more incredible than that a materialized spirit's words could be heard when whispered at a distance of a few inches in the ear of a mortal, or uttered in the hearing of a numerous assembly. But both are daily and hourly demonstrated facts.

Having therefore had the spiritual telegraph and telephone in practical operation long before we learned of the processes of Morse, or Bell, or Daguerre, Spiritualists may claim priority in discovery ; and as no information about the spirit world can be relied on from anybody *except some one who has been there and come back to tell*, we hold that if our informants are honest, we can take their testimony as confidently as we can the accounts of Livingstone or Stanley, about life in the Dark Continent.

If this be so we can see no more difficulty in learning about the domestic life which our spirit friends are leading there, than in the case of the Esquimaux at the Pole, or the Negroes on Lake Tanganyika.

We may, for the moment, be imposed on by a Baron Munchausen, or beguiled by the fiction of a De Foe ; but a thousand counterfeits never made good coin bad, nor bad coin good. The coarse and bungling counterfeits of impostors in Spiritualism, should be dismissed as worthy only of punishment or contempt. The lying spirits in all things, are ever with us, and therefore the greater need of "trying the spirits."

It is only in this spirit of candid investigation that new truths can be discovered or accepted. The universe of unknown facts is never revealed to the Bourbons of the race. Men who never forget the old, never accept the new.

A striking instance of this occurred recently in the case of Rev. Heber Newton, of New York, in one of his brilliant and learned lectures on the legends of Genesis. While speaking of angels' visits to men in patriarchal times, he well said that "there may be other and higher beings than men, and communications may well be made from the spiritual world to human spirits in the human form, and these tales may be only the poetic forms of such spiritual experiences, as come to us in our own age-experiences, whose reality we are as yet neither prepared to affirm nor deny."

XXIV.

WHAT I HAVE LEARNED OF OUR RELATIONS TO THE SPIRIT WORLD.

1. IN all communications which I have received or observed concerning the occupations of the inhabitants of the spirit world, I have always been struck with their pre-eminently *human character*. In no respect have I on any occasion heard a sound or seen a form that did not bear the unmistakable qualities and marks of our common humanity, nor have I ever met a Spiritualist who did not say the same thing. One and all consider all spiritual apparitions and sounds and acts, as originating in human beings who have passed away.

This is the most reasonable and philosophical conclusion to which any clear-minded person can arrive. This will account for all alleged spiritual phenomena, and it divests them of all that ghostly mystery with which vulgar superstition has clothed them.

When young persons—as in the case I described of the lovely girl from Jamestown—are allowed to see a returning mother as though she had just come home after an absence, she is recognized with affection and delight, and there is nothing to cause fear or distress.

All children should be brought up in the same way. Nobody can tell how much misery ghost and hobgoblin stories have unnecessarily produced in the minds of children who are thus cruelly victimized to the ignorance and superstition of mothers, nurses, and servants. No child properly brought up would ever be afraid of *the dark*.

2. *The naturalness of the spirit life* is a lesson which all returning spirits teach, and which we should teach to our children. Even the most ignorant and besotted fathers tell their bereaved children that the mother is not dead, but gone to a beautiful country which is called heaven, and that she will greet her loved ones when they go to live with her.

This is the creed of every religion under heaven, and every creed sanctions so holy a belief. The descriptions brought back to us of the future life of the blessed by the departed of all nations, and all divine revelations, and above all by our own loved ones, represent heaven as peopled by human spirits called angels, who become guardians of the living. More than any other religion, except the faith of Spiritualists, does Christianity inculcate this, and it is a poor and a spurious Christianity which makes war on Spiritualism because it claims that its believers profess to hold more intimate communion with the redeemed than they do or can themselves.

They get their ideas of a future life as they have been taught by traditions a thousand or two thousand years old, and served up into six hundred hydra-headed wrangling sects and creeds; while Spiritualists derive their belief directly from those now living in the spirit land, who return and talk with those they knew and loved, identifying themselves here as plainly as they ever did in flesh and blood. From such persons and sources alone can we get any reliable or exact information about the

future state, or the condition or pursuits of its inhabitants. The one class accept a transmitted
belief with, at best, only a shadowy fabric of evidence, while the Spiritualist reposes securely on
the solid foundation of demonstrated facts.

An interesting case of materialization without
the presence of a known medium occurred at
Montreal. Ten years ago seven young ladies at
a Hallowe'en party agreed to meet on the tenth
anniversary at the same house, and it was stipu-
lated specially "dead or alive." The originator
of the plan and the pledge suddenly died. But
the six survivors, who had preserved a vivid
memory of the agreement, met again in the same
apartment, and a chair draped in black was placed
where the deceased girl had sat ten years before,
and on the table in front of it was a cluster of
withered flowers taken from the grave of the departed one.

The lady who had sat next to her at the first
meeting, experienced a strange nervous agitation
which she could not suppress, but after a while it
passed away and was almost forgotten. After
tea this young lady started for the parlor, leading

the party, and carrying the withered flowers in her hand. On opening the door she was suddenly arrested, and pointing at some object before her, they all saw a tall white figure standing in the room which none of them doubted was their old friend and companion. It disappeared. But the principal lady opened the door into the hall, and her cry brought the whole party to her, when they all exclaimed, " It is she again ! " for they saw the same figure once more as they had seen it at first. The street door seemed to open of itself, from which the figure vanished, when the door closed, apparently by no mortal hand.

3. Nothing that purports in our times, or in previous ages, to reveal to mortals the occupations of human beings in spirit life, is more clearly announced or proved than that they carry with them the same proclivities and tastes they had cultivated or indulged in here. For no other pursuits are they prepared, and as their education in this mortal state is only preparatory to the future, this education naturally goes on, and continues in an endless career of advancement.

As there is no opportunity for the indulgence of

any sensual lusts and passions in a spirit state, all their occupations must be confined to the realm of the intellect and the affections.   Avarice no longer finds its gratification in accumulating gold, for there is no gold there ; nor can any other of earth's material possessions add pleasure or consideration in a sphere where they can carry no weight, since they have no place.   Man takes with him no treasures but those which belong to the intellect, and the soul.   These alone are spiritual, and the spirit's possessions alone are enduring.

There the soul asserts her majesty and rules supreme.   Lazarus and Dives change places.

So it is not surprising that those who have most cultured the intellect and the affections, enter at once upon the new condition with immense advantages in the race for eternal life.   They go right on—the rest have to wait till they can begin to learn the alphabet of how to live.   They find it a hard life.   They all tell us so.   It is all natural and all right, and they would have been fortunate had they known it before.

The student who dedicated his mundane existence to learning the laws of the physical universe, at once yields to his master-passion, and seeks and finds his congenial place. It will be in the company of his old masters in science and learning, who will open to him new fields for knowledge. The astronomer will look for Newton, and Copernicus, and Kepler, and Galileo, and resume his studies anew. The poets will all inquire for Shakespeare, and Dante, and Homer. The inventors will find Arkwright, and Fulton, and Watt, and Stevenson. The engineers will ask for Archimides, and the painters and sculptors will find their way to the palace studios of Phidias, Michael Angelo, and Raphael. There is no limit to the spirit world nor to the pursuits of its inhabitants. There the true and the good will all find endless fields for the occupations they are best adapted to, and in which they will take the highest delight.

When asked, a few evenings ago, about the life the departed lead, spirit Holland, one of the best known and best beloved of a vast circle of Spiritualists in New York, responded:

" We lead active and real lives. Our homes are natural and tangible ; indeed, so much so that to the newly arrived one, it is for a time difficult for him to believe that he has made the transition. None but returned spirits can set the world aright in regard to God, and the laws of the universe of matter and mind. My Christian friends, the whole fabric of your dogmatic theology is fast melting away before the sunrise of truth which is beginning to shine into human hearts. It may seem to come slowly. But the demands of suffering humanity for spiritual food are so much greater than the supply, on account of the lack of a sufficiently large number of qualified mediums to answer the wants and aspirations of the light-seekers, that spirit-workers are pressing their forces through every mediumistic avenue which is open to their approach.

" At all our *séances* a double work is carried on : the materializations which you all witness, and the unseen development of mediumship and spirit-work, produced by harmonizing and blending for co-operative effort the spirit-hands of mediums who are present. The children of Spiritualists are not taught that they can receive the benediction and instruction of the angels outside of the *séance-*

room, while they *should* be able to realize that spirit guardians and friends are with them *at all times* and *in all places*.

" Circles for spiritual instruction and unfold-ment should be formed in every household. In the atmosphere of the loving emanations of the home circle, the heart is warmed and opened to influx from the spirit spheres, and both parents and children can then be approached by those heavenly teachers who are often debarred from public *séance*-rooms by the clashing, antagonizing elements of suspicion and distrust. Instruction thus received at home from spirit teachers, would be of incalculable benefit in all the duties and temptations of their after years."

From another speaker of a spirit band we re-ceived the following reply to an inquiry about the *manner* of spirit life :

" As spirits we can realize all sensations through our master-sense—*perception ;* as when looking on mortals we can see the events of their past lives. The motives for right seem to illumine the soul's aura with indescribable brightness, and cast a halo of beauty over the whole being. 'Do you see that old man?' said a spirit pointing to a person in the *séance.* 'He has not a comely look to mortals; but as a soul in the light of his noble life, the emanations that he casts forth are like those of an angel.'

"I could tell you many things which are revealed to the soul's eye but unknown to the bodily senses. I feel sure that human beings would shrink from crime, or even bad thoughts, if they knew how hideously they show on the soul. Crime can be wiped away only by personal, not by vicarious atonement as taught on earth. The world will soon learn far more about all these things, for the spirits are preparing to bridge over the gulf more effectually, and men and spirits will soon cross and recross it familiarly.

"Every spirit has a home, a place, where all one has loved and wished for becomes embodied in the soul's surroundings.

"We teach that man as a perfect organism cannot die. The mould in which he is formed must perish, in order that the soul may go free.

"Humanity *must* move on. It is ordained that the world *must* finally attain to a true knowledge of spiritual existence.

"Physical science has conducted the world up to the gates where spiritual science commences. The world *must* grow, and Spiritualism is one of its outgrowths. As men grow into spiritual light, they better understand the methods of communication.

"The earth is full of occult forces. Trees and plants, minerals and fluids are all teeming with magnetism ; to draw them forth and to apply them will be the next phase of science which humanity will achieve.

"You ask, ' Is the soul a substance ? ' I heard some one put this question. I answer, Is the air or wind a substance? You cannot see or feel either until they come into contact with some other substance ; but when they do, although invisible, you know they are *something*. The soul is something finer than the atmosphere—finer than ether, and it can pass through matter with perfect ease.

"You also inquire ' how bodies in which spirits return, and the clothing they wear, *are made?* '

"It is a difficult question to answer so that you will understand it, but perhaps not more so than for one of your chemists to explain the aroma of the rose, or the difference between its perfume and that of a hundred other varieties of flowers ; or account for the transmission of the poison of disease through the atmosphere sometimes by a single inhalation, or the growth of vegetable fungi in an hour, or the rending of a sturdy oak into splinters, or a granite cliff into fragments by a lightning bolt in a small part of a second. All you know is *the facts.*

"There are numberless physical phenomena constantly going on before your faces and eyes which your chemists cannot explain ; and so there are elements and forces in air, water, and solid substances of which science is still ignorant, and for which chemistry has no name. Even of the names of ascertained elements, the mass of mankind are ignorant. It ought not to be thought very strange, therefore, that spirits should not be able to answer all questions. They are not possessed of all knowledge ; only the Creator Spirit has infinite knowledge. In these respects there is no other law or process for the acquisition of knowledge among spirits, than among mortals.

Experience, study, observation, and *the help of teachers:* over this road all created beings have had to travel in the past, and will have to pass forever. This is what alone can be called *the royal road to learning.* You have all degrees of this on earth—original endowments by nature, opportunities more or less favorable, and circumstances more or less auspicious for embracing them; and all through life what you call good or bad fortune, of which no two of you seem to share alike; so that all these things account for the endless diversity of earthly conditions.

" Very much so, you must think of spirits in their spheres. The differences are not so great in some respects, but in others they are vastly greater. Ignorance, and especially mental ignorance, is slow of illumination; but spiritual and indurated ignorance is slowest of all.

" As concerns the clothing of the returning spirit body with substances which will identify its personality and its costume, and how it is all attired, this is the clearest explanation we can give. We say then :

" *First,* we must have mediums present gifted

with those capabilities of attracting the elements necessary for us to use in clothing our spirit bodies, so that we shall be recognized by those who knew us as mortals, and when we are able to appear successfully, we are always attended by spirit chemists, who either help us or teach us in this work. Thus after more or less training, some of us are able to come alone, although we are seldom unattended.

" *Second*, we must not only have this mediumistic reliance, but we must have a harmonious circle, with no hostile or antagonistic elements present. These discordant influences are fatal to all peaceful social circles even among mortals ; how much more so among spirits—you know what the ' still small voice ' means.

" It is under such conditions that we have our best successes. You must not be astonished at the quickness with which our preparations are made, for your own electrical discoveries have ab-'solutely annihilated space and time, and if you have compelled some of the occult forces to do your bidding as mortals, can you wonder at the power of the immortals ? "

XXV.

INFANTS IN SPIRIT LIFE.

THE question of the future condition of departed infants, of whom so many millions pass away every year, had often interested me, and lately so deeply as to create in my mind some anxiety, for reasons which I need not explain. I was shortly favored with the following communication, of which I transcribe the substance and spirit, and for the most part, the exact words. It was an advanced spirit who spoke, and she seemed very desirous to have her message as widely known to American mothers as possible :

" We have no children *born* in the spirit world ; our spheres are replenished only from the earth. We take them up, one by one, as they press on us from a world of which they could have known so little, and of the mysteries of existence they could have had no conception. This is one of our most sacred *duties*, as well as one of our most delightful engagements.

"Infants who come over, grow with great rapidity, and with none of the hindrances or drawbacks which so generally—if not universally—impede their perfect development on earth. You must not suppose that we consider it fortunate to die early, for it was designed by the Infinite Father to have his earthly children learn by experience how to save, enjoy, and prolong mortal life to so mature a period that the transition to a higher life should occur without shock or pain; and with some, this does happen. It will become more common as men learn the laws of nature, and the inevitable penalties attached to their violation. And yet we never forget, when we clasp the tiny new-comers to our bosoms, that they have been safely landed on the shore of deliverance, where none of earth's troubles will ever reach them. They are all safe here.

"Oh! if earth's mothers could only see with what tender care their dear ones are watched by their *spirit mothers*, how different their feelings would be at the period of their bereavement. The love of the *earth mother is great indeed;* but it can hardly surpass that of the *spirit mother* for her adopted child. As soon as one of these little ones reaches the higher life, the arms of a thousand mothers are opened to receive it ; and how many of these prematurely cut-off ones are wisely saved from evils to come, unseen even by the immortals ! No one can tell.

" When they are old enough (as you say, or sufficiently developed as we say) they go to school, and there they are furnished with the best facilities we can provide for their advancement.

" All Americans ought to know who our beloved Margaret Fuller was—that great and noble woman who was so great a loss to earth, and how much greater gain she was to us. She is engaged in teaching a great school for young girls, of the most brilliant capabilities for the highest achievements in the future. She had surpassed most of her contemporaries in higher knowledge while she lived in mortal life, and now since finding her place here, she has had full scope for indulging her ruling passion—the elevation of her sex to the position which the Supreme Master intended her to occupy, in his sublime development of the final destinies of the earth.

" Only a few of her associates knew how amply Margaret Fuller was endowed with those spiritual qualities which elevate them in our world.

" And lest my strength, or your time may fail, let me say to every earth mother that, though her dear one may have passed over to our side when it was only in the tenderest of infancy, yet that mother's heart will recognize it at once, when they meet, though it may have grown to manhood, or bloomed to beautiful womanhood before her arrival; for the ties of *true affection* formed on earth remain unbroken here.

" Also I may say that mothers who have left infants behind them, are so engrossed in the old love and care, that were there not a law of nature to compel them to stay a part of their time in the spirit world, they would pass every moment with their children. Each one, however, is compelled to learn her lesson of progression.

" There is work here for all hearts, and all hands. This is not confined to our friends alone. Some of it must be given *to our enemies*. They are among the first ones that we seek, for if we have done them any wrong our duty and desire is to atone for it, which the transgressor alone can do; and if one has done us wrong, the injured one alone can touch the heart of the wrong-doer by carrying to him the olive branch of forgiveness and love. Love is the only instrument of power we can use here. With that alone can we win the dwellers below us, and elevate them to higher spheres. If this is the greatest power on earth, how irresistible must it be in the spirit world!

"Mortals, especially the mass of the undeveloped and the sensual, think so little, and really so thoughtlessly about immortality, and put it so far away from them, that it is, as you know, very hard to get them away from the sordid lives they lead. But as soon as they recover from the blind, half-dazed entrance to the lower spirit sphere for which alone they are prepared, their minds begin slowly to open to the reception of the new light. That is the stage where they feel their helplessness, and after a while they begin to grow willing to learn from kind lips, lessons which fell upon deaf

ears, even when, if ever they were, uttered lov-
ingly, in the midst of their earthly degradation.
Of this work we never grow so tired that it becomes irksome, for we see our progress, and it
furnishes us a never-failing reward."

In giving such impressions to my readers as I
have received from my spirit friends about the
lives they lead in their present homes, I should
never forgive myself if I had neglected to tell how
infants and young children who die early are received, and treated in the future life. It would
seem that if any communications from the departed should interest the living, it would be for
mothers to know about their little ones who have
been laid away in the cold ground, forever beyond
their sight. Thank God we are not left here without intelligence, which should bring comfort to
every bereaved mother's heart.

Among all the clear and satisfactory messages
which come to us from the Better Land, none are
clearer or more comforting than these :

From the earliest dawn of life, some guardian
spirit is assigned to watch over it throughout its
mortal career, and this guardianship never ceases

till its final emancipation in being born into immortality, which is its second birth.

It is the business of this guardian spirit to attend its charge constantly, to save it from every danger to body or soul, and do for it the best that can be done during its earthly career.

If it is taken away in tender years, it is not cast aside like a waif, to drift helplessly on the dark ocean, but borne in safe hands into a peaceful and beautiful home, where it is guarded and guided by tender and loving ones, shielded from all the troubles and temptations of earth, and developed into the higher and blessed society of the celestial spheres. This can be done only by the spirits of departed mothers, sisters, and relations of the young immortals who are numbered by millions in the annual flight of our earth around the sun.

What spiritual vision can grasp so vast and sublime a spectacle, or conceive the extent of the field of these tender ministrations? How long this process has been going on, we neither know, nor perhaps should, if told, be able to comprehend. But of the truth of the revelations made known to us, we have the most abundant demonstrations.

The signs, moreover, of still broader and more intimate relations between the material and the spiritual world, are multiplying throughout the earth. They are not confined to one or more nations, or tribes, or families of men ; but as might naturally be expected, the progress of spiritual knowledge corresponds in equal ratio to the advancement of science and virtue. Hence, we find these two sources of knowledge are everywhere seen going hand in hand, and marching side by side. All finite beings, mortals and immortals, obey the same organized law—to seek for light.

This is the chord which vibrates through the ages, and in tracing it backward as transmitted to us by the sages, and forward to its connection with their more highly illuminated minds in higher spheres, we can readily account for the amazing progress of scientific knowledge in our own times, and we are thus prepared for still more astonishing discoveries in the future.

Beliefs have done little good for mankind in the past, and incalculable evil. Ignorance can boast of no achievement except as the fruitful mother of superstition, and her children's bones have whit-

ened the soils of dead empires. Science has carried the only torch which has illuminated the human pathway, and inspiration has been her only
guide. To this celestial source all the great bene-
factors of the race have, through all historic time,
bowed in humble and devout adoration. The
freed spirits of the sages of antiquity from Homer
and Socrates, and Plato to Pythagoras and Con-
fucius, and so down the ages through the unbroken line of light-bearers, till we reach our days,
when we hold in our hands the golden skirts of
an age of universal illumination.

XXVI.

COUNCILS IN THE SPIRIT WORLD FOR MUN-DANE INFLUENCE.

ON this subject I have been favored with communications which I esteem to be of higher importance than almost any others I have received, since they seem to come from more advanced spirits, and they inspire me with higher hopes for a far more rapid and brilliant development of the spiritual dispensation on earth, than we have hitherto expected.

But if I did not feel that these messages were as clearly and satisfactorily made as those simpler ones of which I have recorded a few in this work, their authenticity would be so clouded by mysticism and doubt, they would find no place in these unpretending pages.

I do not suppose that the economy of this system of intercourse between the earthly and the spiritual worlds admits of the messages of the advanced spirits reaching us as directly, and demonstratively to our bodily senses, as when they come to us so familiarly from our recently departed friends. But I am fully convinced that those higher spirits can, and do, transmit to us, through the mediums of lower spheres, such impressions and inspirations as they wish to have reach us.

1. From what little I have learned on this subject, I am firmly convinced that no knowledge of a future state is communicated to mortals any further than they are prepared to receive it. It could not consist with the economy of the universe to waste any of its resources, whether material or spiritual, in vain attempts to hurry results before their time. Hence, in our limited knowledge, we are often liable to grow so impatient as to incur the hazard of missing what we seek, by trying to realize it before it can come. This often happens in our mundane affairs. How much more necessary to cultivate that serenity of mind which alone can inspire the patience that wins the prize at last.

All experienced observers of spiritualistic phenomena know how easily they are interrupted by disturbing the harmony of a circle through the presence of a hostile, or even an uncongenial person. The same effect is seen in the execution of delicate music, or a jar in forming crystals in a laboratory, or any sudden shock in genial social circles. So, too, it often happens that the most astounding displays of spiritual power in physical manifestations often occur in dark circles; and in thousands of well-authenticated cases of ghostly apparitions, and strange noises, in so-called haunted houses and places. Ask the chemist how many of his finer processes have to be conducted only in the dark. The secret may be too subtle for his perception, but he knows *the fact.*

For all my readers I wish to emphasize the important idea—especially to those who are examining into Spiritualism for the first time—that they would do well to approach this, like any other subject, and accept the facts as they come, and determine them by the same evidence by which they settle all other facts. I have acted in this way, and I do not yet learn, or believe, that we should now, or hereafter, expect that any other law of thinking, or acting, would be adapted to the human reason. By this, and this only, can the intellect of man ever be approached. One, and only one, law for mortals or spirits.

2. As we move on from this life to another, these laws prevail; and we shall undergo no change in the spirit life that will ever metamorphize us into anybody but ourselves —we shall preserve our identity forever. Otherwise, there would be chaos in the universe, which is an impossibility in this great Cosmos, in which no exception has yet been found to impair the perfection of its unity, or the supremacy of its laws.

Of course, there must be grades of progress there, as here. Advancement by progress is the law there, as here, in everything that belongs to the universal system of the *groundwork*, and the *development* of the first idea of the Creator and Author of it all. The details of the work, must correspond with the final consummation, which no created being is able to comprehend.

But through the mediumship of the departed who have known the earth, we may, and do, get their experiences as far as they have advanced, and this knowledge is now being communicated to millions of the living. This is more or less fully known to those who have taken the necessary steps to acquire it.

3. But some have taken the trouble in this case, as in so many others, to go further, and in response to their aspirations they have gained more light—direct or reflected—from upper spheres. Just as perseverance and study reward the seeker for higher knowledge here, in any of the occult domains of nature.

4. But we must come to superior light to know something beyond these inferior things which more immediately concern what I have been attempting to unfold. Thus far I have confined myself chiefly to our *immediate intercourse with our personal acquaintance*—those whom we know have passed on to the spirit world, and recognize when they return. They tell us what we can readily believe, that in their young life *there*, while they can give us no very extended experience of a spiritual condition, yet through some of them who were better prepared for that life, they

were found more ready for admission to a more
exalted sphere than most others, and they could
tell us something that would give us no uncer-
tain glimpses of the more elevated circles above
them.

And of such sources of information we are fully
assured. Of the many occasions which we might
cite for such a conviction, I can, with well-assured
confidence, give the following as a clear, if brief,
representation of the progress going on in the
spirit world, toward the grand consummation they
are making for the advancement of the earth's inhabitants to a higher condition. ·

5. As might readily be supposed, we find that
groups of sympathetic spirits should unite to devise the most effectual plans for their earth work,
and arrange necessary measures for carrying them
into effect. These groups, or councils, are as
numerous as are the diversified interests, classes,
and pursuits which concern mankind, and in
which, during their earth lives, they were themselves engaged.

It is impossible to conceive how any system
should prevail there, entirely different from the

one which prevails here, and throughout the physical creation as far as we see or learn—— *Aggregation* of mutually attracted units into aggregated wholes, as worlds of matter were formed ; or the *concentration of minds*, for the achievement of some common purpose. All power is multiplied by the aggregation of units of forces.

6. As a consequence, we understand that there must be a complete organization of all spiritual circles of individuals who assist at their consultations. Old as our world seems to be, it has only reached in recent times its present stage of evolution. The agencies of steam, electricity, and the only faintly developed powers of magnetism, had to become known to men before departed spirits could begin their great work in ushering in *this New Dispensation.*

All through the preceding ages, earlier earth-emancipated mortals shot occasional gleams of light on the paths of the most favored of men, among all nations, and they did their best to raise their fellows up to higher conditions here, and higher aspirations hereafter. But they could only succeed far enough to kindle the fires which kept the world so long from utter darkness.

But these lamps are now burning in more places around the earth than ever, and shedding a brighter light. The widely scattered families of the human race are coming closer together, and beginning to think and see more alike. When this work is complete, the *present mission of spirits* will have been accomplished.

What may lie beyond the present, which is never given to mortals or immortals to do, is not revealed. It is enough for all the children of earth here, or in the upper spheres, to know that all created beings, like all things else, are advancing —as fast as they are prepared—for higher and still higher stages in the never-ending spheres of existence.

Said an advanced spirit to our last circle before this record closes:

" Cherish the words we have given you. Follow the light you have, and new light will fall on your path. We have trod wearily the same road, but have gone through safely, and we pledge you our sacred assurance, that our birth-world shall hereafter grow brighter and better as the years go by.——Farewell dear ones—Farewell !! What nothing else has yet been done for our poor suffering earth, is to be done by *the New Dispensation*—SPIRITUALISM ! "

XXVII.

SPIRIT MEDIUMS.

THIS large and rapidly increasing body of persons, are being better understood, and consequently more respected. They have existed in all ages. In some countries they have suffered persecution and death. In others they have been regarded with the highest reverence, particularly among the Greeks and Romans, whose Oracles and Temples were specially dedicated to the business of revealing the future, and forecasting the fates of men and nations. For the most part vestal virgins, or other females, were chosen for this work, because of the acknowledged delicacy and susceptibility of their sex. Much superstition was mixed up with customs and beliefs from the Jews down to the witchcraft days of Puritan Salem.

But the diffusion of light is substituting truth

for error, and knowledge for blind belief. The relations between mortals and immortals are the same, Spiritualism is the same, and mediums are all the same ; but the whole system is vastly more developed, and infinitely better understood.

This is due chiefly to *mediums*—by which term I designate those through whose organism—and for reasons we cannot explain—spirits are able to communicate with mortals. We have the facts by the million, and we accept them, and act upon them, just as we do on a million of other facts which the most learned cannot explain.

If there were not pretended mediums, so-called, it would be very strange in a world so full of liars, counterfeiters, thieves, hypocrites, and the endless tribe of deceivers who waylay the unwary at every turn in life.

But there is less danger from false mediums than from their brother and sister villains in other nefarious trades, from the church to the banking house—they are sure to be detected sooner or later—generally very quickly ; for every true medium, and every true spiritualist, must be their enemies and detectives.

There seems to be six classes of clearly defined Mediums, who are now chiefly engaged in spreading the knowledge of the truth of positive and assured intercommunication between us and our departed friends.

1. The *first* class are *Trance Mediums :* Those who appear to lose their self-control, and in this state of somnambulence, or physical insensibility, speak strange words, as though they were messages which seem, or profess to come from doubtful or incredible sources. And yet so many things of this kind are known, that they no longer excite much painful surprise. On the contrary, their words have afterward been found to convey most important intelligence.

2. The Psychometrists, or soul readers, who can portray another's thoughts, whether present or absent, and convince either that they have the power to do this. This power has so often been displayed, that it has long ceased to be doubted among multitudes of the most careful of examiners.

3. *Inspirational Speakers.*—The American rostrum has, for many years, presented innumerable

instances of lecturers who have, at unknown and unsuspected occasions, been asked to discourse on subjects of more or less importance, and who, to all appearances, could have had no time for preparation, and the discourses indicated a convincing, logical train of argument, and elevation of thought which would have honored the highest efforts of human genius. Hundreds of such addresses have been pronounced before promiscuous assemblies, containing eminent orators, acute lawyers, and learned men, who had no words to express their surprise and admiration. They could account for what they heard and saw, only by " something they could not understand." Spiritualists could understand it all, by tracing it to the agency of higher beings, who have in all past time breathed their inspiration to the leaders of our earth who have sought light and inspiration from higher sources.

4. Another class are Physical Mediums, who seem to be but passive instruments through whom purely physical results are attained—as we use musical instruments, such as ordinary manuscript writing on paper, slates, artistic work on drawing

paper, bells, pianos and guitars, etc.   All done in presence of a medium, but not by the medium.

5. *Healing Mediums,* by whom marvellous cures of bodily infirmities of every kind are effected, and those wonderful restorations to health and life, which have been in past time, and are still, accomplished.

6. And, finally, the most astonishing of all displays of spirit power on earth—*the full form Materializing Mediums.*   Here the most skeptical have to yield, for they see and test the demonstrations made not only to their intellect, but their bodily senses.

XXVIII.

LAST ANNOUNCEMENTS FROM THE SPHERES.

ONE of the most astonishing and pleasing displays of spirit power I ever witnessed, occurred between Christmas and New Years, 1883–84.

It was strictly a private *séance*. Only myself and two gentlemen, scientists and personal friends —Dr. Gross and Professor J. Jay Watson—whom I had invited, were present. The doors were securely locked, the cabinet thoroughly examined, and the gas from the chandelier burning brightly. No possible precautions against deception or mistakes were neglected, and all that happened had to pass the severest scrutiny.

After some exquisite music on the organ by Professor Watson, the curtains opened, and in our full sight, five materialized spirits appeared. It

13

was the first time that I had seen more than one
spirit form appear at a time. These were all
arrayed in flowing robes of pure white. They
folded the curtains back, and closed them again,
two or three times, hesitating, as if to gain strength,
but came out again in clear view, and responding
to our recognitions, returned their salutations and
vanished into the invisible air.

I tried to imagine what any sceptic could say
who saw that sight !

Some time before, at another *séance*, spirit Holland had promised me (I dislike to use this egotis-
tic pronoun so often) a surprise, and I felt that he
had made good his pledge. But something more
was to come.

After the five spirits had vanished, the curtain
again opened, and spirit Holland appeared with
his daughter Angelica on his arm. This was her
first materialization at this cabinet. She was a
beautiful spirit, and looked quite as tall as her
father. I was called to the cabinet and presented
to her by her father. In my presence he placed
his arm around her neck, and kissed her with the
touching affection of a loving father.

Dr. Gross was next invited to approach, and he remained in conversation for a while.

After this scene passed, many of our dear friends appeared and talked with us individually; all known and loved, and each one recognized and perfectly identified.

One spirit in particular approached, and taking my arm walked with me all round the room. In passing by Dr. Gross, she placed her hand on his head, and addressing a few kind words to us, we walked back to the cabinet together, where she also vanished from our sight—not *behind the curtain*, but into air.

Then came a spirit who seemed to be one I had known some years before, and who had, through another medium, identified herself as she alone could do.

During my attendance at the *séances*, I heard mention made of a spirit who often appeared at the circle wearing, over a white dress, a long black scarf. This spirit afterwards proved to be my friend who committed suicide, as I was told, in consequence of an unhappy marriage. On this occasion she appeared all in white robes, and radiant with joy.　She called me to her, and said, loud enough for every one to hear :

" My good friend, if you had not been in Europe at the time, that sad event would not have taken place.　But that black scarf has become a thing of the past with me.　You will never see it on me again.　Thanks ! thanks to the Great Father of all ! I have passed out of that terrible mistake of my earthly career, and now I can pass to a higher life."

She then called up another person in the circle, and said :

" See !　Look !　The black scarf is all gone ; all things are now new with me.　Bless you all."

She then passed into a soft clear light just as the curtain was falling.　Spirit Holland appeared and said to us :

" We do not intend to say anything about the spirit that has just gone ; but what a lesson it teaches to earth children !"

Among the most pleasing and satisfactory surprises that come to us, is intelligence from the Spirit World about the manner in which some of our friends are received on their arrival at their final *home.*

I use that word *home*, because it best conveys the idea which our friends give us of the rest which the weary and heavy-laden experience, when they fully know that they have escaped from all the uncertainties and vicissitudes of earth.

They who have lived here, have gone through it all, and they know best how to tell the story of their life *beyond*.

We often have occasion, in our earthly experience, to remark the difference which the departure of one person and another excites. By simple intuition, all beholders felt alike as the body of the beloved Peter Cooper was borne by ; and not one in a million of spectators but felt that he, at least, had gone to the home of the good if there were any life hereafter. So, too, with all such men whose virtuous lives endeared them to the race.

Among my contemporaries of this class, whose fame rests on the enduring basis of devotion to the good of humanity, few have left a better record than Dr. Marion Sims, the great American surgeon. I knew and loved him. It so happened that on the day while the bells were tolling for his funeral, at the *séance* we were privately holding at my own house, we received a startling and most affecting message of the manner in which the intelligence of his departure was received in the Spirit World; and we were favored with a vivid description of his reception there.

I can almost give the very words of the celestial message :—

" More than one of the upper spheres had been prepared for his approach, and heard of his departure from earth with simultaneous joy. We all went out to meet him in groups of kindred spirits, bearing fruits, and floral offerings, and celestial music. We attended him to the home which his good deeds had built and embellished for him ; and after seeing his weary spirit reposing in charge of those who had known and loved him best on earth, our anthem of praise softened into silence as we withdrew."

XXIX.

PARTING WORDS TO MY FRIENDS, OR STRANGERS, WHO ARE NOT SPIRITUALISTS.

I CANNOT know now, nor perhaps ever, what effect this litttle volume may have on the living, nor on those who may come after us. The future is in the hands of the Infinite Being, of whom I am but a loving child. I can only say that I have, in writing it, done my best to shed a ray of light on the clouded pathway of some who may, through it, be guided into clearer and more cheerful prospects of the endless future.

That Future! It is, after all, what oftenest absorbs our most secret, our most sacred thoughts, especially when alone. The creeds, the theologies, the philosophies, the theories, and even the dreams, do not answer the questions we ask ; they do not satisfy the aspirations in which we so often indulge, and which we must cherish. We wonder! What then can we do ?

What then ?   That question comes—it will come for an answer, and if we would find *peace*, we *must* get the response.

Do the old oracles tell us ?   Do their responses satisfy us ?   Do we fall to sleep so soon, or so sweetly, as we should if we *knew* something more *definite*, more *positive*—something *certain*, *real*, *absolutely sure* about the future, as we should be glad to know ?

No ! No ! I early trod that road.   It gave me no certainty ; and it left me miserable—for I did not *surely know where I was going. Faith* did not satisfy me : *I wanted knowledge.*

That knowledge I found, and it has been a source of so much comfort to me, that I would not part with it for all the wealth of the earth.

I did not write this poor little book for Spirit- ualists alone—they know all the lessons I attempt to teach ; but I wished to win some others to the CLEAR LIGHT which beams on us, only *from the* SPIRIT WORLD.

And so I dismiss this little work, to the care of the spirit friends through whose inspirations I feel that it has been written.

KATE IRVING.

FINIS.

www.ingramcontent.com/pod-product-compliance
Lightning Source LLC
Chambersburg PA
CBHW030829020726
47499CB00006B/2128